Lost in HOLLYWOOD

Also by Cindy Callaghan

Just Add Magic

Lost in London

Lost in Paris

Lost in Rome

Lost in Ireland (formerly titled *Lucky Me*)

Coming Soon

Sydney Mackenzie Knocks 'Em Dead

Lost in HOLLYWOOD

CINDY CALLAGHAN

Aladdin M!X

New York   London   Toronto   Sydney   New Delhi

This book is a work of fiction. Any references to historical events, real people, or real places are used fictitiously. Other names, characters, places, and events are products of the author's imagination, and any resemblance to actual events or places or persons, living or dead, is entirely coincidental.

ALADDIN M!X
Simon & Schuster Children's Publishing Division
1230 Avenue of the Americas, New York, NY 10020
First Aladdin M!X edition August 2016
Text copyright © 2016 by Cindy Callaghan
Cover illustration copyright © 2016 by Annabelle Metayer
Also available in an Aladdin hardcover edition.
All rights reserved, including the right of reproduction
in whole or in part in any form.
ALADDIN is a trademark of Simon & Schuster, Inc.,
and related logo is a registered trademark of Simon & Schuster, Inc.
ALADDIN M!X and related logo are registered trademarks of Simon & Schuster, Inc.
For information about special discounts for bulk purchases,
please contact Simon & Schuster Special Sales at 1-866-506-1949 or
business@simonandschuster.com.
The Simon & Schuster Speakers Bureau can bring authors to your
live event. For more information or to book an event contact the
Simon & Schuster Speakers Bureau at 1-866-248-3049 or
visit our website at www.simonspeakers.com.
Cover designed by Jessica Handelman
Interior designed by Hilary Zarycky
The text of this book was set in Goudy Oldstyle Std.
Manufactured in the United States of America 0716 OFF
2 4 6 8 10 9 7 5 3 1
Library of Congress Control Number 2016939148
ISBN 978-1-4814-6572-4 (hc)
ISBN 978-1-4814-6571-7 (pbk)
ISBN 978-1-4814-6573-1 (eBook)

To Kevin: I'd be lost without you.

Acknowledgments

In addition to the Academy, I'd like to thank . . .

First, my awesome writing partners: Gale, Carolee, Josette, Jane, Chris, and Shannon, and the Northern Delaware Sisters in Crime group: John, KB, Jane, June, Chris, Janis, and Kathleen.

And thanks to my friend Leo for inspiring the whole Burrito Taxi business!

A special thanks to my USC friends for e-mailing and texting me details when my memory failed me, which was often. I hold my time with all of you in LA in a special place in my heart.

If I could pick two people to stick on a Velcro wall with me, it would be my literary agent, Mandy Hubbard from Emerald City Literary Agency, and my editor, Alyson Heller. Thanks to you both for your continued support!

Of course I would never venture down the red carpet without my loves: Kevin, Ellie, Evan, and Happy.

Most of all, thank you to my readers, to librarians, and to teachers and parents who read and recommend my books. I hope you love *Lost in Hollywood* as much as *Lost in Ireland*, *Lost in Rome*, *Lost in Paris*, *Lost in London*, and *Just Add Magic*.

A girl knows her limits,
but a wise girl knows she has none.
—Marilyn Monroe

Lost in HOLLYWOOD

1

I'm a totally normal thirteen-year-old girl. For real.

The problem is that I'm surrounded by weird.

Dad said, "Come look at this one, Ginger."

He was talking to me. I'm Ginger. I'm named after one of my mother's favorite old movie stars, a lady named Ginger Rogers. (Mom is totally obsessed with old movies.)

I walked over to see my dad's latest contraption; he makes things out of stuff.

I looked at this Saturday's gizmo. "What is it?"

"I call it, the Drool-o-Dabbler."

"Uh-huh." He had taken the chinstrap off my little brother's football helmet. FYI, Grant—who's also named after an old movie star—doesn't use the helmet for football.

He tapes balls of aluminum foil to it to help him connect with aliens who might try to talk to him. Although they never actually have; he does it "just in case."

I told ya—surrounded by weird.

Anyway, Dad took the chinstrap and melted it to pipe cleaners that he'd bent like candy canes. Then, he stuffed the cup of the chinstrap with wads of gauze, like from a first aid kit.

Dad hooked the pipe cleaners over his ears. "You can wear this to soak up your drool while you sleep . . . or . . . I suppose, while you're awake, if you're the kind of person who drools when you're awake. I would imagine there are people like that. And it keeps your pillowcase dry, or your shirt, if you're awake."

"I guess it would come with extra gauze pads," I pointed out

"Replacements? Sure."

"It's . . . ah . . . great, Dad. This could be TBO." He was always looking for The Big One (TBO). While I agreed there might be people who drool a lot in their sleep—and maybe even some when awake—I wasn't convinced this was TBO, but it always made my dad smile when I told him that.

"I'm gonna need you for the video."

"Of course." I am always in the video. Usually my part in it said, "You know what you need?" Then I would say to someone, usually a part played by Grant, "You need a Drool-O-Dabbler."

Grant would ask, "A Drool-O-Dabbler? What's that?" Then my dad would introduce the product and an online bidding war would begin. "War" is a bit of an exaggeration. The highest bidder buys the Dabbler. The craziest part is, there are always people who want his stuff.

"Just let me know when we start filming," I said, and went to let Grant know about our next acting gig.

I knocked and opened his bedroom door. Until just recently, his room used to be *our* room, which was wrapped in posters of UFOs and extraterrestrials. I just had to get out of there. My new room is very pink and neat. I picked out every single thing in it: lamp, curtains, beanbag chair, etc. . . .

"Greetings, Earthling," he said.

I rolled my eyes. Some girls have brothers who burp; some have brothers who punch them. I have one who thinks he's parked at my house temporarily while he's between intergalactic voyages.

Yay me!

Payton and I have said that Grant will be our first patient.

Payton, btw, is my BFF and future business partner—we're going to be brain surgeons.

"You're needed for an internet video later," I said.

"I comprehend."

"No duh. Not like it was complicated," I said. I didn't know if Grant actually had a shortage of brain cells or if he had some type of cerebral condition that contributed to his whack-a-doodle behavior. I was about to harass him more when the phone rang. I ran to the kitchen to grab it.

"Hello. This is Ginger Carlson," I said. One day I'd have someone who would answer the phone for Payton and me: "Hello. Dr. Ginger Carlson and Dr. Payton Paterson's office."

"Hello. My name is Leo. I'm Betty-Jean Bergan's housekeeper. Can I talk to you about her?"

This guy thought I was my mom. Probably because I sound so mature. People always tell me that.

"Uh—" I tried to interrupt, but didn't succeed.

"Your aunt has had another incident. It was serious. Dude, I don't know what to do about her."

I asked, "What do you mean *another* incident?" *And why is he calling me (or my mom) dude?*

"Oh, my bad. I thought your hubs told you. I spoke to him the other day . . . about her behavior. It's strange, odd, Halloween without the candy. And today, well . . . she fell."

I gasped. "Is she okay?"

"Get this, she wanted to climb the Hollywood sign," Leo the housekeeper said.

"*THE* Hollywood sign? The big famous one?"

My mom's aunt Betty-Jean (or ABJ as I call her) lives in Hollywood, California. She's my coolest relative: she's beautiful, used to be an actress, and lives this totally glam life in Hollywood. I've always wanted to visit her, but she comes here instead of us going there. At least she used to; it's been about three years since I've seen her. I never understood why she would want to come to Delaware when she lives in California.

"There's only one Hollywood sign," Leo continued. "She's out of the hospital, and they said she's gonna be okey-dokey, hunky-dory, A-okay, but there's something else. A sitch."

"What kind of sitch?" I asked.

"The money kind. She has none: zip, zero, piggy bank empty." He paused. "The bank wants to take away her house."

I gasped again. "Her home? That's terrible!"

"You're telling me. She asked that I call you to see if the family would come out here and help her."

Out There? As in Hollywood? For real? Obvs I wanted to go to LA, and my mom, the classic movie nut, would totally love it. Dad always says he has to work, but if ABJ needs him, I bet he'd take time off. I mean, he finds time to make contraptions, right?

"I hope you do come because she doesn't only owe the bank money, if you know what I mean."

I covered the mouthpiece and yelled to Mom and Dad in the living room, "ABJ's housekeeper is on the phone. He says that she fell off the Hollywood sign! The bank is taking her house!! So we need to go to Los Angeles to help her!! Can Payton come?! Next week is spring break!!"

Mom rushed away from the TV—something she only does for a pee emergency or a grease fire. "Let me have that." She snatched the phone. "And please stop yelling." She took the phone out of my hand. "Hi, sorry about that. Okay. Uh-huh. Uh-huh. Yes. We'll be there." She hung up. Now Dad and Grant joined us in the kitchen.

Mom said, "My aunt Betty-Jean needs our help. Get ready. We're going to Hollywood!"

2

Dad arranged to take the week off from work, so the whole family was going. And Mom confirmed that I could invite Payton, as long as her parents said okay.

"ABJ is your aunt, which makes her my great aunt?" I asked Mom. "She doesn't have a family of her own, right?"

Mom nodded. "She never got married or had kids. She was always so busy with her acting," Mom explained. "You know, she's the reason I love old movies."

"So, she's on her own out there, in Hollywood?" I asked.

"Well, she has friends and Leo, but no family other than us."

Payton flew in the back door without knocking, which is nothing new. We have that kind of house, and Payton is that kind of friend. On the other hand, when I ride my bike to her house, I knock on the door, she has *that* kind of house. "Are you sitting down?" she asked.

Mom and I gestured at the stools we were sitting on at the kitchen island.

"Oh good. Six words: Airplane miles. Free trip. Payton coming." She jumped up and down. "My parents said okay!"

My eyebrows jetted up to the ceiling. "That's perfect!" Going to Hollywood would be awesome. But going to Hollywood *with Payton* would be better than awesome. I asked Mom, "That's perfect, isn't it?"

"Absolutely."

"I know. Right?" Payton asked. "I feel like I'm one of the family." She held up a tote bag. "And you know what's in here?"

"I bet I do." I ticked off a list on my fingers. "Model Magic, paint, notecards, thin-tipped Sharpie markers, thumbtacks, toothpicks and. . . hmm . . . chocolate?"

Payton closed her eyes and smiled happily. "Eeeeexactly."

Mom asked, "What's all that for?"

We yelled at her, "The Science Olympics!"

"It's right after spring break," I added.

"We're making a model of the brain," Payton said. "Of course."

"We're totally gonna win," I declared.

"We *have* to."

"We made a bet with the DeMarcos," I said.

"They're twins," Payton added.

Mom followed our conversation back-and-forth like she was watching a Ping-Pong game. This is how Payton and I speak. We've been best friends since we were babies and we spend every spare minute together, so we pretty much always knew what the other was thinking. Not that we're telepathic, because that doesn't exist, although some scientists think that communication using only thoughts is within our reach, but if it did, we'd have it.

"The DeMarcos are making a robot," Payton said.

"How cliché," I said.

We rolled our eyes in sync.

Mom hates listening to us when we talk like this. (She calls it "chat back.") She put her hands over her ears. "Stop it, girls. You're giving me a headache."

Then Grant came in wearing his football helmet with aluminum foil balls. He poured a glass of milk, squeezed in strawberry syrup, and stirred. Then he grabbed a Twizzler, and instead of eating it, he used it as a straw. "Good stuff," he said smacking his lips. Tucking a roll of aluminum foil under his arm, he left.

I said, "His weirdness gives *me* a headache." I slipped two Twizzlers out of the bag and gave one to Payton. "Doesn't it bother you, Mom?"

"He has an active imagination. He's nine. It's normal."

"Do you think it's normal?" I asked Payton.

"Sounds like a family matter," Payton said. "I'm staying out of it."

"I thought you said you were part of the family," I teased.

Mom said to Payton, "You know while we're in California, you'll have to help with Grant too."

"No problem, Mrs. C," Payton said. "I'll hide in the closet, and in my alien voice I'll whisper that we're sending a spaceship to get him."

I laughed. "Good one." We high-fived by tapping our Twizzlers together. We'd come up with a million different ways to high-five without using our palms.

"No," Mom said. "Not a 'good one.'" She snatched our Twizzlers, and with one bite nibbled on them both. She smiled. "But a little funny."

3

⟳

The cab drive from LAX (that's the airport in Los Angeles) was traffick-y. There were ten lanes of superhighway, five in each direction, and all were packed with cars. If the highway was the central nervous system and the cars were oxygen, there would be seriously bad neurological consequences, like brain damage.

It was also seriously bright out, and I had lost my sunglasses at the bottom of my bag. Luckily, Payton handed me her very cool aviator shades; they looked oh so Hollywood. Speaking of Hollywood, *hello, palm trees!* I'd never actually seen one in person, but they were everywhere, and they looked just like you'd think they would from their pictures.

"We need a teleporter," Grant said, staring at the traffic. "Intelligent life on other planets teleport all the time. I'm sure."

I whispered to Payton, "I'd like to teleport him back to his home planet."

Mom said, "I heard that."

Dad sat in the front seat gabbing with the driver about his driving-related gadgetry needs. He gave the driver a card with his website address. Then he gave him a second card in case he needed life insurance—that's my dad's *real* job.

As soon as we got off at the exit marked HOLLYWOOD, my mom started snapping pictures. "This is Sunset Boulevard!" CLICK. "It looks just like it does in the movies. There's the Sunset Tower." CLICK. "And—oh my gosh! Oh my gosh! THERE IT IS! Pull over." The taxi slowed until it finally stopped on the side of the road. "Do you see it?" CLICK. CLICK. "It's the Hollywood sign." CLICK. CLICK. CLICK.

Like palm trees, I'd seen pictures of the Hollywood sign, but I had to admit that in the hazy sunshine, the letters in the distance, way up on the hill, were amazing. Even *I* clicked and—*swoop*—sent it to my QuickPik page. If it isn't on QuickPik, it's like it didn't really happen.

"Birth mother, can we please go now?" Grant asked out the window, squinting.

"I'm your only mother." She got back into the cab.

"We don't know that," Grant said.

I said to Mom, "I think he's giving you permission to put him up for adoption."

Mom ignored me. The cab maneuvered through the city streets, and the CLICKs started again at the approach of the Beverly Hills sign. Mom said, "Look down the streets." CLICK. "Look at how every street has only one kind of tree. How interesting." CLICK. "And not a garbage can anywhere." CLICK. "Where do you imagine they put their trash?" CLICK.

"You know, we're going to run out of room for all the trash," Grant said. "And you know where it will go then? Space. We'll attach it to a space shuttle and just drop it somewhere. Space litter. That's what it'll be." Somehow he wasn't worried about the junk in my former bedroom. "Unless it can be glued together into some kind of lump."

These are the kind of brain things that fascinate me. At nine he has to wear Velcro sneakers because he can't learn to tie the laces, but he can solve the issue of space garbage while driving through Beverly Hills.

"Do you think we'll have intergalactic trash pick-up people?" I teased. "Like, is that a job of the future?"

"We'll need someone to gather the trash lump, like a . . . a . . . an Interstellar Waste Engineer, to prevent a hazardous outer space situation. That person would need to know about planetary orbits and gravitational forces."

He can't tell when I'm teasing him. It takes some of the fun out of it.

CLICK.

Dad scratched a note on the little flip pad that he always keeps in his shirt pocket. "There are a lot of invention needs for trash right here on Earth," he said. "Like lids, for example. They blow off and fall to the ground and get run over. I should be able to make sure they stay on the can." He jotted on the pad.

I wondered, not for the first time, if this was my real family. Maybe I'd been switched at birth—somewhere there was a family of doctors with a daughter in a space suit watching old movies while doodling inventions.

4

Aunt Betty-Jean's house was nestled high up in the Hollywood Hills. The houses around it were more like bungalows. In comparison, ABJ's was huge.

"Only one person lives here?" Payton asked about the two-story flat-roofed house with floor-to-ceiling windows.

"Just Aunt Betty-Jean," Mom said.

"It's wonderful," I said. "Look at all those windows!"

A man who didn't look like a housekeeper or butler, but more like a fifty-year-old surfer with unshaven, tanned skin; sun-bleached hair; a woven parka; and sandals, let us in.

"I'm Leo," he said. "Welcome to Hollywood! Although, I wish you were visiting for a better reason."

Mom gave him a squeeze. "So good to meet you in person."

The first thing I noticed when I entered the house was a huge painting of ABJ. She looked beautiful in a long red dress, wind blowing in her hair, which was blond like mine.

"She's totally glam," I said, pointing to the painting.

Mom said, "She looks like Marilyn Monroe in that picture."

"Check this out." Payton ran her hand along a sculpture that nearly hit the ceiling. "Maybe it's by a famous artist."

"Maybe it was custom made especially for her," I said.

"And maybe it has some existential meaning to it," Payton said.

"And may—"

"I'll take your luggage, dudettes," Leo interrupted.

Once we got past the painting, the house was a little less glam. It was too warm, and smelled like stale popcorn and Mexican food. Sunlight tried to sneak in through the windows that were thick with grime, filling the room with the same type of haze that cloaked the Hollywood sign. (Leo must not be a very good housekeeper.) There were curvy sofas that may have been elegant in Marilyn Monroe's time, but now they made the place feel more like a vintage furniture store.

"She's in the master bedroom suite." Leo pointed. "Over yonder."

We walked across the living room's white marble floor to the bedroom, which was hotter and stuffier than the rest of the house, but just as big and similarly decorated in a retro style. It had a sitting area, a bathroom, and double doors that probably led to a closet.

ABJ's appearance surprised me. Her eye was black-and-blue and a bizarre shade of green. A bandage wrapped around her head disturbed the flow of her lovely hair. Despite the wound and medical cloth, she still looked elegant in red lipstick a wearing a satin robe.

"Hi, Aunt Betty-Jean," Mom said. "How are you feeling?"

"My head hurts." She rubbed the gauze dressing with a manicured hand. "And that nurse won't give me any aspirin."

To Mom Leo whispered, "I've worked for her for eleven years, so she knows I'm not her nurse, but in the afternoon things get foggy, mucky, guacamole in the head."

Foggy isn't enough? Foggy and mucky aren't enough? He has to add guacamole to her head?

Mom said to ABJ, "I'll get you some aspirin."

"Thank you, doctor."

"Umm . . . I'm not your doctor. It's me. Sue. Your niece. Your *only* niece."

She looked at Mom with a blank stare. Then her eye twinkled a smidgen. "Right. Of course," she said. "I'm just playing with you, Sue. Sue the Salamander. That's what I used to call you, right?"

Mom relaxed. "That's right."

"I'm tired now, Sue."

"Of course you are." Mom pulled ABJ's sheets up under her chin. "I'll see you a little later."

ABJ looked past all of us to Payton and said, "You were always my favorite, Ginger."

Now, since I haven't seen her in a while that might not have sounded so strange, *if* Payton and I even looked a teeny tiny bit alike. But we don't. We're similar in height and we wear the same size jeans, and we both wear pink shoes whenever possible—it's like our signature—but there's one big very noticeable difference in our appearance. Payton is black, and I'm white. So, this was a very strange thing for ABJ to say.

Once we were outside of ABJ's bedroom with the door closed, I said, "Wha . . . wha . . . *what* was that?"

Payton said, "Two words: Whackytown."

"I think that's one word," Mom said.

Payton ignored her. Payton knows how to count words. She does this sometimes to be funny, but other people don't always get it. Not everyone understands our academic or science-y humor. I'd grown to expect it.

Then Payton added, "Maybe we've spent so much time together that we actually *are* starting to look alike. I've heard that happens to people who are married for a very long time. And some people start to look like their pets."

I took her by the hand and led her to a nearby wall mirror. We stared into it. I never thought of my bestie in terms of a color. To me she is just Payton, or Payt. "I think most people can probably tell us apart." I lifted my foot. "Unless you only look at the kicks."

"Yup." We always seemed to agree.

"You look like a space worm," Grant said to Payton.

"There's no such thing," Payton said.

"Just because you haven't seen it, doesn't mean it doesn't exist. Exhibit One—the tooth fairy."

"Let it go," Mom said to Payton, who was ready to debate the existence of the tooth fairy with Grant.

We walked back over to Dad, who spoke with Leo just

outside ABJ's door. "What did I tell you?" Leo pointed to his head. "Guacamole."

That certainly wasn't a medical term, but I got the gist of what he meant.

He continued, "I hate to suggest it, because I love that woman like she was my own mother, but maybe she needs to be in some kind of a hospital or special home."

"She isn't *that* old," Dad said.

"Well, tell her brain that, because it's crumbling like a taco shell in a blender." Leo walked over to a pile of mail on a tabletop supported by a pair of carved ostrich legs. He handed a bunch of official-looking documents to my dad. "Look at these."

"They're from the Los Angeles Police Department," Dad said.

"That's right. The po-po have rounded up ol' Bette a few times. If we don't get this figured out, she's gonna end up in the big house, the clink, Club Fed." Even though Leo had used three different descriptions, we must've still looked confused. "Jail!" he said. "Let me know how I can help." He crossed the marble floor and left, pulling the front door closed behind him. It slammed loudly. Then he opened it again and said, "Sorry. That was the wind. I didn't mean for it to slam like I was making a dramatic exit. I'm not the angry sort. Peace out."

Grant said, "Soon we're gonna run out of room to put criminals and we'll have to exile them to another planet. Probably Mars. They'll be our test colony to see if human life can survive there. Near Mars's equator it can be seventy degrees during the day, so that's no problem, but it's negative one hundred degrees at night. It should be interesting to see how our species evolves."

Payton tapped the side of Grant's head. "There is a lot going on in there. It's a shame we can't channel it to something . . . Earthly." To me she said, "He may be a candidate for a partial brain transplant."

"Yeah," I said. "The part that makes people normal."

We high-elbowed on that.

"Well, she doesn't *look* so bad," Mom said.

Dad said, "I think there's more going on than a fall. We need to get her to a doctor."

"I'll make an appointment," Mom said. She glanced around at the grandeur of the house, reminiscent of the 1940s, or maybe it's the 1950s. "I wonder how much money she owes for this house."

"Wasn't she famous?" I asked. "Doesn't she have lots of money?"

"She was, so I guess she did," Mom said. "Unfortunately, she hasn't had an acting job in a long time. Look at this place. She probably spent it all."

"She could've thrown it into the Pacific," Dad said, "and not remember."

"We'll talk to the bank first thing tomorrow." Mom opened the refrigerator door. "I think I'll run to the store, by way of Hollywood Boulevard, of course, where I'll also pick up one of those maps of the star's homes. Maybe there'll be time for some sightseeing while we sort this out." Then she said, "You kids put on your pj's. The bedrooms are upstairs." As she closed the fridge she scanned the magnets. "Look at this ad. It's for Burrito Taxi. I don't know what that is, but Aunt Betty-Jean loves Mexican food. Let's give it a try. I can go shopping tomorrow."

"Anything with a burrito is cool with me," Dad said.

While Mom used her cell phone to text an order as directed by the magnet, we went upstairs to find everything covered in white sheets. There wasn't much up here for Leo to clean, which made me wonder what that man did when he came to "housekeep."

Payton and I chose a room with twin beds. The bedroom set was the same style as the rest of the house—maybe new age. If Dad was making an Internet video to sell it, he'd say it was in "mint condition," because it looked like it had never been used.

There was a knock on the front door. We looked down the center staircase to see Leo standing in the foyer in a taxi-cab-yellow-and-black-checkered shirt and hat. There was a fabric burrito attached to each shoulder.

"Did someone order a Burrito Taxi?" he asked.

5

"You're a housekeeper *and* you drive a Burrito Taxi?" Dad asked.

"I *own* a Burrito Taxi," Leo explained. "I deliver people and burritos. I keep all the ingredients hot in the trunk. You text me what you want and I'll drop it off. I drop off people too. And I pick them up. I don't pick up burritos."

"Very interesting business model." Dad scratched his head. I'm sure he wished he'd thought of it.

"Yup. And all profit. I won the taxi in a contest, so there are no payments." He pointed to the street. "Go check it out."

We rushed to the door and looked out. It wasn't any kind of normal taxi. In fact, it was so far from normal that

I wondered for a minute if Leo was a distant relative of ours—well, the rest of my family, not me.

"It was in a movie," Leo said. "I did the artwork myself."

All the paint in the world couldn't hide the fact that the Burrito Taxi was a banana vehicle. That is, it was a working car shaped exactly like a banana, but painted like a burrito with its stuffing oozing out the sides and end—black beans, rice, cilantro, guacamole. Leo was clearly a right-brained person—that's someone who is good at art and has an active imagination—not unlike Grant, and Dad. Payton and I used our left brains more in our word of logic and facts. I'd put Mom somewhere in the middle.

The Burrito Taxi had two doors, one for the driver, and one for the passenger. Both seats were very low to the ground at the center of the banana . . . err . . . burrito. The front and back ends of the taxi bent up in a banana-like shape.

"I started selling banana splits—they melted," Leo explained. "Then bananas on a stick—they browned. And then I thought . . . burritos! People in Hollywood love burritos! Now they could have them delivered. No one else is doing that. And since I have the passenger seat and a little backseat, I had extra room for people. Most people don't mind the ride taking a few extra minutes to stop for a delivery or two because they love making an entrance somewhere in a burrito."

"I like the way you think, Leo," Dad said. "Do you have a passenger out there now?"

"Oh yeah. Yup. *Sí.*"

"Who?"

"My very own teen business manager in her traveling office," Leo said.

"Where is she?"

"On the other side."

We hustled out and around the opposite side of the burrito mobile. There was a plexiglass dome with strips of green plastic streamers resembling shredded lettuce hanging from it.

"A sidecar," Dad said. "You just don't see those enough anymore."

"And," Leo pointed to brackets, "it's removable."

"Genius," Dad said.

A girl wearing headphones and tapping at an iPad slid a small section of the plexiglass aside like it was a window at a take-out place.

"¡Hola!" She was dark-haired and tan. "*Mi nombre es Margot.*"

"Oh," I said. I knew enough Spanish to introduce me and Payton. "*Mi nombre es Ginger. Y esto es Payton.*"

"¡Hola!" Payton shouted, like the girl was hard of hearing.

I said, "Payton, she speaks Spanish. There's nothing wrong with her ears."

"Oh right. Silly of me." Then she shouted real slowly at Margot. "*¡¡Cómo estás?!*"

"*Estoy bien*—uh—" She pointed to the headphones and pulled a little microphone attached to a wire to her mouth. "*Hola. Burrito Taxi.*" She listened. "*Sí. Sí. Diez minutos.*"

Leo said to us, "My niece Margot is about your age. She's spending her spring break helping me out. I told her she doesn't have to, but she loves me and she loves this taxi. She helped me paint it, you know." He lowered his voice. "But, if she had a few pals to hang with . . . then, I wouldn't feel so guilty. Maybe you girls can, you know, do whatever it is girls do?"

"Gotcha," I said, but I was thinking that it might be a little difficult since she didn't seem to speak English.

"It'll be fun," Payton said. "We girls stick together. It's like a big club."

27

"ABJ was right about you. You *are* great." He looked at his watch. "I gotta go. Places to go. Burritos to deliver." He looked at Dad. "You coming?"

"Heck yeah!" He looked at my mom, then asked Leo, "I mean, can we swing by the grocery store too?"

"No *problemo.*"

Mom said, "You never go shopping."

"I never had a Burrito Taxi sitting in the driveway."

"Okay. Don't forget milk and eggs and take Grant," Mom said.

"Can he fit?" Dad asked.

Leo put his hand on top of Grant's head. Then he lifted him and put him down. "He can fit in the back."

Just before they left, Mom asked Dad, "Can you get me a map of the star's homes?"

Dad winked at her, then got in front.

We waved as the burrito mobile and its sidecar pulled out of the driveway and then we went inside.

Mom took two burritos and went to ABJ's room.

Payton and I brought ours upstairs and ate in the bedroom. "Is that genius?" I asked her. "Or crazy?"

"I was wondering the same thing. Maybe some of the craziest ideas *are* genius," she said. "What about the first time someone suggested lettuce in a bag? Maybe people thought *that* was crazy."

"Maybe one day all taxis will deliver Mexican food," I suggested. "Or—"

"Kittens!" we said together.

We really do think alike.

6

The next morning Payton and I came down the grand center stairs in matching pink high-tops. I paired mine with a white miniskirt. My long blond braid bumped off the middle of my pink T as I walked.

We found ABJ and Grant sitting at a small table in the breakfast room, which was like a casual dining room off the kitchen. It had big French doors that opened onto a patio, from which you could see the whole valley that was Hollywood. Grant was hunched over a handheld game, his thumbs moving lightning fast.

ABJ's bandage looked like it had been rewrapped around newly coiffed hair. She flipped through a copy of *Entertainment Weekly* and nodded along as Grant explained, "The trash will need to be gathered into a lump . . ."

"How would you keep the lump together?" ABJ asked.

"Gorilla Glue."

"You'd need a lot."

"Oh yeah," Grant agreed, still not lifting his eyes from his game.

My mom and dad, freshly showered, came in to get coffee from the pot on the glass table and filled travel mugs for themselves.

"How's your head?" Mom asked.

"Much better, dear, thank you."

"We were going to talk to the people at the bank today. Do you want to come? I can drive," Mom asked ABJ.

"Oh, thank you, but I'll stay here."

"Are you sure?" Dad asked. "It might do you some good to get out."

"No thanks. I don't know who may call or stop by and I want to review a script that I got in the mail."

"Okay." Mom offered her a paper. "If you don't come, you'll need to sign this, so that they'll talk to us about your financial matters." Mom used to be a lawyer, so producing official papers in a snap is easy peasy for her.

ABJ slowly scrolled her signature with a big loop in the J in Betty-Jean, like an autograph that she'd given a million times, which I guess it was, although maybe not a million. ABJ had one big role that she won an Oscar for in the 1960s. Besides that, she'd had only small parts in small movies.

Leo walked in the front door. "*Hola*," he called. He came into the breakfast room, and to ABJ he said, "You're up. And looking like a superstar." To us he asked, "Doesn't she look fab?"

"No, I don't," she said and pretended to push away the compliment with a little blush.

"Leo, we're going out for a while," Mom said. "To look at Aunt Betty-Jean's financials."

"Do you want me to take you in the Burrito Taxi?" he offered.

"Sure!" Dad cried.

Mom placed her hand on his shoulder. "That's okay. Aunt Betty-Jean is letting us use her car."

"The Caddy?" Leo confirmed with a look of surprise. "She never lets *me* use her Cadillac."

"Maybe she likes me more?" Mom teased.

"Don't know about that," Leo said. "I always have a supply of shredded cheese. The ladies like a guy who travels with cheese. Know what I mean?" He nudged my dad who nodded and laughed along, but I don't think he understood what Leo meant. Neither did I. "When I saw that Cadillac, I immediately thought, 'mega long hot dog deliveries.' Not just hot dogs, of course, also kielbasa, sausage, bratwurst, anything long that you could put on a bun. That car is so big, it could hold a six-foot dog nicely, you know?"

"Oh, I know," Dad said. "What do you say, Aunt Betty-Jean? You want to go into the mega jumbo long hot dog business? It could be the answer to your every financial worry."

Dad and Leo, I suspected, would be friends for life.

"Can I get back to you on that?" ABJ asked.

Dad said, "You take as much time as you need."

"But how would you buy six-foot buns?" Mom asked.

"*That* is a problem," Leo said. "But I think this guy"— he poked my dad—"could find a solution for that." Leo was probably right.

Mom said to Leo, "We should be back around noon." To me, Grant, and Payton she said, "Stay out of Leo's way. He's not your babysitter."

"Payton and I will start on the Science Olympics." I turned to ABJ and explained, "A model of the brain."

Payton said, "We're using clay."

"And we made a bet," I added.

"With the DeMarcos."

"They're building a robot," I said.

ABJ said, "How cliché."

We all laughed.

ABJ's brain seemed totally fine, even sharp, this morning.

Mom interrupted. "Girls, you'll give her another headache doing your chat back."

"It's okay," ABJ said. "I haven't seen Ginger in so long. I love to hear her voice." She put her hand on mine, indicating she knew which girl was me. "And tell me your name again?" she asked Payton.

Payton told her and the two went through the basic introductions again. As Mom and Dad slipped out the door, a hand emerged from nowhere and stopped it from slamming behind them.

Margot appeared, headset on, wire microphone bent to her mouth, and she was listening to an order, "Sí. Sí." She handed us burritos while she spoke.

ABJ told us, "Every morning Leo goes out to his car and makes a different kind of breakfast burrito. Margot is helping this week. Have you seen his car? That man is a genius."

"Wonder if he can lump space trash," Grant said, more to himself, his eyes stuck on his game.

A cell phone rang and Margot said into the wire mic, "*Hola.*"

Leo topped off ABJ's coffee. "I need to check our supplies. I'll be right back," he said. Then he added, "I hope your niece has luck at the bank." The door slammed behind him. He reopened it. "Sorry! It was the wind. I gotta fix this thing." And he closed it again, more gently that time.

Margot noted on her iPad what the person on the phone was saying.

"Your mom won't have luck at the bank," ABJ said to Payton and me.

"What do you mean?" Payton asked.

"My money isn't in the bank."

"Then where is it?" I asked.

"Did you spend it all?" Payton asked.

"Or maybe you gave it away," I suggested.

"Or maybe you—"

"No." ABJ looked over at Margot, who looked like she was listening to someone on the phone. "I have to tell you a secret."

We leaned in to hear.

"Okay. You see. The money. I hid it," ABJ said.

"You *hid* it?" we asked together.

She nodded. "*That* is why I needed you to come out here to help me. I knew your mom and dad wouldn't believe me, so *you* . . ." She looked right at me when she said this. "I knew you would help me."

"Of course. Anything," I said.

"I hope you like adventure," ABJ said.

"We love adventure. Right, Payt?"

"Love it," she agreed. "But what does an adventure have to do with the money?"

ABJ whispered, although I'm not sure why; no one except Grant was around to hear her. I mean, Margot wasn't far away, but she was listening to a customer. "Like I said, the money is hidden. I need *you* to find it."

"Where's it hidden?" I asked.

"Somewhere in Hollywood."

7

⌣⌣⌣

"Okay, but . . . *where* in Hollywood?" I asked.

She took a piece of paper that looked like it had been folded and unfolded a million times out of the pocket of her long satin bathrobe, palmed it, and slid it over to me.

I glanced at Margot, who still appeared to be involved with someone on the phone. I unfolded the paper. Once it had been square, but now the bottom right-hand quarter was missing.

"What's this?" I asked.

Payton pointed to a doodle. "What does this mean?"

"I can't make out what it says," I said.

"Your handwriting is terrible," Payton added.

ABJ reached across the table and put a hand over

each of our mouths. "Your mom wasn't kidding about your chatty bat."

Grant, still completely focused on his handheld game said, "Chat back. They're always like that. Annoying, isn't it?"

"Jeesh. Yes." She pointed to the paper. "This is where I hid the money; I think. And, I think, my awards."

"You think?" I asked.

"The problem is, sometimes I forget things. I think I left myself this clue to remind me where I hid it. Isn't that what you would do if you were hiding your life's savings?"

I guess that made sense.

"But you aren't sure?" Payton asked.

"Like eighty-nine percent sure."

"That leaves eleven percent," I said.

"That's not much," ABJ said. "Almost single digits."

"What awards?" Payton asked.

Staring at his game, Grant answered, "ABJ won an award called an Oscar, and a few others, the Félix and the Julio. Julio is spelled with a J, but it's pronounced like 'who.' Who-lio."

"Some of that is correct," ABJ said, but didn't elaborate. "I can't find the awards and I can't find the money. I know I

38

took it out of the bank, because I was pretty sure they were stealing from me and I wanted to hide it, but I couldn't decide where. Then I found that note."

"Stealing the money right out of your savings account?" I asked.

"Can they do that?" Payton asked.

"I don't think they can, but I think they did," ABJ said.

"So you hid it? Like a pirate," Payton confirmed.

"Eighty-nine percent sure. And that's where things get foggy." She sighed. "If I don't find it and pay the bank the money I owe them, I'm going to have to come to Delaware to live with you."

HOLD EVERYTHING.

Margot finished her phone call, but I hardly noticed because I was focused on the bomb ABJ had just dropped.

"Would you like something to drink?" Payton asked Margot. "¿Agua?"

"Sí. Gracias," Margot said. She leaned over Grant's shoulder to watch the play-by-play.

Quick math: Our house has four people and three bedrooms. One of those people just got her own room. (It's pink, by the way.) The nine years prior, she'd shared a room with an outer space oddball. But now she had her own girl cave. It was Dad's former workroom. (Now he works in the garage, and parks in the driveway).

If ABJ moved to Delaware, I knew which room would be hers.

And I knew who'd be back in an interstellar nightmare, on the bottom bunk.

Payton gave Margot a bottle of water from the fridge.

No. No. No. That was not going to happen. I was going to do everything I could to help ABJ stay in her own home, which she clearly loved—in Hollywood.

ABJ added, "I love you guys, but I don't want to leave Hollywood. If I leave, and the Academy of Motion Picture Arts and Sciences can't find me, I'll never know if they want me to have a star on the Walk of Fame."

"They could find you in Delaware," Payton suggested.

"What if they don't bother and just go on to the next person?"

"Is that how it works?" I asked.

"They have a list and go down it and find people?" Payton asked.

"Are you on the list?" I asked.

"Or maybe you have to apply," Payton suggested.

"Maybe there's an interview," I added.

"Maybe an audition," Payton said.

"Maybe—"

"Girls." ABJ closed her eyes and put her hand on her head where she had the bump. "Please stop."

"Sorry," we said.

She opened her eyes and said, "All my stuff is here. This is my home."

8

~~~

Payton and I grabbed our breakfast burritos. I was going to invite Margot to come upstairs with us, but she started pointing to Grant's game and making noises like my dad makes when he's watching football. She seemed like she was having fun, and it would be a shame to disturb her.

We spread out on one of the twin beds and studied the paper that was worn from being handled. On the top left corner there was clearly a big block letter *D* with an arrow pointing to something that would've been on the section that was missing. Then there were thirteen—like straight lines on a hangman game—across from left to right. The last dash was darker than the others.

On the bottom left corner there were a bunch of tick

marks with slashes through them. They reminded me of little bales of hay.

Then at the bottom right corner it said:

Hidden in a famous place that few know.
They look at it, but don't see.

Payton asked, "How can it be famous, but few people know?"

"I don't know. Maybe a famous place, but a part of it that no one goes to? You know how you go to museum or something and there's a piece of art that no one looks at?" I asked.

"I went to a wax museum in London, Madame something, and there was a whole room of historical figures," Payton said. "No one even went in. Everyone wanted to get their picture taken with the wax celebrities."

"Wouldn't you?" I asked.

"I know. Right?"

I took the first bite of my breakfast from the Burrito Taxi. The receptors on my tongue got a clear message that was sent to my brain—spicy, eggy, cheesy, warm, and shockingly good.

I swallowed. "There's a wax museum here. Maybe we should try it."

Payton took a bite, and without swallowing said, "Feels like a needle in a haystack."

I pointed to the paper. "But we have a *D*. Maybe a wax figure with the name starting with a *D*. Or a middle initial *D*," she said. "Maybe this arrow was to a drawing of someone—a face."

"Now you're thinking," Payton flipped open her Mac-Book. "I'll make a list of wax people we should look at." She licked her fingers before typing.

"How would they hide money, though? And an award?" I grabbed a tortilla chip that came with our breakfast. Speaking of delicious, *Hello, chips.*

"The award could be ABJ's actual award, but people *think* it's wax. Like, it could be hidden in plain sight—*People look at it, but don't see,*" Payton said. "And the money?"

"That's harder. Maybe the wax figure isn't solid—"

"Like a hollow chocolate Easter Bunny," Payton interrupted.

"And it's stuffed with money," I finished.

Payton paused from her typing and took another bite while I chipped both hands.

Why don't I have chips for breakfast at home? I thought.

"I already have some names. Snoop Dogg, Judy Garland as Dorothy from *The Wizard of Oz*, Robert Downey Jr. as Tony Stark from *Iron Man*, Dwayne Johnson, and more."

"Dorothy carries a big basket. And I think maybe a suitcase too. They could be full of money." I started getting excited.

"Or wax," Payton said.

"More likely it's wax, right?"

"Right," she said.

"But things are not always how you expect. I thought these burritos would taste like the back of a banana car. But they're great," I said. "Maybe the best I've ever had."

"I know. Right?" Payton said. "And these chips. You think he has a deep fryer in the trunk?"

"He's got something in there."

"What else could be a famous *D*?" Payton asked.

"There are all those stars' names in the sidewalk. The Walk of Fame. Tons of names there."

"Good one." She typed a note. Grease shined off the laptop's keys.

"Or it's not a name. Maybe it's a place," I said. "Like . . ." I asked my phone for a list of famous places in Hollywood. "The

Dolby Theatre. Don't know what that is, but it's famous and a *D*. The Museum of Death—"

"Eeew," Payton said.

"Yeah. Let's skip that one." I tried to get some of the grease and salt from the chips off my hands.

"The Hollywood sign?" I asked about what I saw Payton typing. "There's hardly a *D* in that at all."

"Um, it's the last letter. Without it, it would be Hollywoo." Then she added, "And it's kind of a major landmark."

"Fine. Add it." Then I leaned over to review the list.

Madame Tussauds Wax Museum

Walk of Fame

The Dolby Theatre

Rodeo Drive

The Hollywood sign

~~The Museum of Death~~

I looked at the list. "It's going to be a busy week."

"It's not even a full week. That gives us today, tomorrow, Wednesday, Thursday, and Friday."

"One hundred and twenty hours," I said.

"To find a buried treasure in a big city," Payton said. "*And* to make the winning project for the Science Olympics."

"We can do it," I said.

"I know. Right?"

"If we don't—"

Payton shut her eyes. "I don't even want to think about losing to the DeMarcos."

"Me either. But it's not just the Olympics. If we don't find the treasure, I'll have to move back in with a freakazoid Captain of the Universe wannabe."

"None of us wants that to happen," Payton said.

"Ya think?"

Payton looked at her empty burrito wrapper. "Think Leo and Margot have more in the trunk?"

9

⊷⊶

"That burrito was amazing," Payton said to Leo. Margot was on another call. She was serious about helping Leo while she was off of school.

"Thanks. My breakfast burrito business has been growing like crazy. In fact, I have a bunch of orders Margot just took. Thank goodness she speaks Spanish."

I asked, "Do you think you could drop us off at the wax museum?"

"As long as it's okay with your mom."

"I already texted her. It is."

"Just let me know when you're ready to go." He took ABJ's coffee cup to the kitchen.

Once he was far enough away, ABJ looked up from the

game of Uno that she and Grant were playing and whispered, "You figured it out? It's at the wax museum?!"

"They're really smart," Grant said.

"Awww. That was such a nice thing to say, Grant," Payton said.

"Too bad that they're ugly," he added.

"And there it is," I said. "You walked right into that, Payt." To ABJ I said, "We didn't figure it out. With that chunk of paper missing, this is gonna be tough, but we have a couple of ideas and"—I looked at the countdown app I put on my phone—"one hundred and twenty hours to figure it out."

"Of course that time is split with the Science Olympics project," Payton said.

"Does the wax museum sound like somewhere you would hide money?" I asked.

"I don't know. I mean, I've been there. . . ."

I looked at the app. "No time to waste, we'll check it out."

"Okay. Good luck." She looked out at the view of the valley that was the glitz and glamour of Hollywood. "It doesn't snow in Delaware, does it?"

Ugh. My beloved bedroom.

"Let's not think snowy thoughts just yet," I said. "Oh,

and I don't think we should tell Mom and Dad about the whole 'hidden' thing."

"Okay. That's what I was thinking too," she said.

"And don't *you* go blabbering," I said Grant. "In fact, just forget that you know."

"Forgetting is easy," Grant said. "*Remembering is hard.*" He played a card that meant ABJ lost a turn and right away he played a second card. "But I would be sure to forget if you were to, say, bring me something from the wax museum."

I sighed. I could've argued with him. But sometimes giving in was easier.

"Like what?"

"Oh, gee, let me think." He tapped his chin like he was thinking, but I knew he wasn't. "Wax! Stupid!"

"Fine."

"In that case, my lips are sealed, unless the question comes from my people." Grant looked up when he said, "my people" referring to his real family who lived on another planet, maybe another galaxy, who knows.

I asked ABJ, "Are we telling Leo?"

"Not yet. I think."

As if on cue, Margot clicked off her call. "*¿Vámonos?*"

"*Vámonos,*" Payton repeated.

Margot led the way and Payton whispered to me, "I think I've used all the Spanish words I know."

We three went to the foyer, where Leo waited. "Is ABJ okay to stay alone?" I asked.

"Sure. She's home alone every day. Never goes out. Always waiting for the phone to ring—someone to call about a part. But no one ever calls and there aren't any parts."

"She went out when she fell down and hit her head," Payton said.

"That's why it was so strange, she never does that. I don't even know how she got there. She didn't drive herself; the Caddy was in the garage."

"She mentioned she was reading a script," I said. "Could that be a new part?"

"She's been reading that same script for six years," he said. "I think she ripped it out of one of her entertainment rags."

"Rags?" Payton asked.

"Magazines," he explained. "People call entertainment magazines *rags*."

"Why?" I asked.

"Don't know. Don't care. And don't care," he said again. He laughed at himself. Seems like he liked to say things in groups of three. In this case, he couldn't come up with a third, so he recycled. And, he thought that was funny. "Anyway, I stop in between deliveries and we have these." He pulled a device as big and clunky as a Bunsen burner out of one of the side pockets of his cargo shorts. "It's a long-range walkie-talkie. She has one too."

"Doesn't she believe in cell phones?" Payton asked.

"She's not a fan of technology." He went back to the breakfast room. "I'm on channel ten," he said to ABJ, then added, "If you're up for it, Sue had her heart set on a tour of the stars' homes."

"This house used to be on that tour." ABJ pouted.

I felt badly for her. "It was probably a pain not to have privacy," I suggested

"And all that traffic," Payton said.

"Traffic is the worst," ABJ replied.

"And the noise," Payton added.

"I do like things quiet, but it's been too quiet," ABJ said.

Leo said, "I'll bet these girls can change that, right, ladies?"

"Totally," I said.

"Just wait till tonight," Payton said, "when we start on the Science Olympics project. We'll turn up the music and make a mess."

I wanted to start the Science Olympics project as much as Payton did, but I thought it could wait until we got this search under control.

ABJ smiled. "I like music."

"But I don't like messes," Leo said.

"Don't worry about that," Grant said. "My mom loves cleaning up messes." He looked at me and Payton. "Can you guys leave? We're in the middle of a serious Uno tournament here."

ABJ added, "He's not kidding. We've bet a treat from Millions of Milkshakes. No monkey business here."

"Fine," I said. "We'll get out of your way."

"Oh, and Ginger," Grant said. "Wax. Or else I might not be so forgetful."

Payton said to him, "I'm starting to understand you better, and now I know why Ginger doesn't like you."

He stuck out his tongue and made a fart noise with his mouth.

We rolled our eyes and followed Leo to the foyer, where we grabbed Margot and headed out the door.

On the way to the car I whispered to Payton, "We're totally gonna check out Millions of Milkshakes."

"I know. Right?" Payton asked.

10

Since the right thing to do after breakfast is to stop for a shake, Leo drove us to Millions of Milkshakes. I sat shotgun while Payton was folded up in the cramped backseat, and Margot was in the sidecar. The plexiglass made me think she was inside a hamster ball.

"Next time we're doing rock-paper-scissors to see who sits back here," Payton whined.

We weren't the only ones who liked pre-lunch shakes because people were already chillin' in the outside seating under the shade of the pink-and-blue striped awning.

"Want one?" I asked Leo.

"Get me a Paparazzi Smoothie. I'm watching my waist."

"You got it," I said. Then I called into a slit of the sliding window of the hamster ball, *"¿Batido?"*

Margot held up a one-minute finger and climbed out.

"How do you know the Spanish word for milkshake?" Payton asked.

"I did an oral report on my favorite foods."

Me, Payton, and Margot went inside.

I thought Leo had been kidding till I saw the menu. The Paparazzi Smoothie did seem healthy—strawberry, coconut, and pineapple juice. But they also had your typical to-die-for ice cream concoctions.

I stared at the menu on the wall. "What are you getting?" I asked Payton.

"Three words: S'mores Shake." She clarified, "I'm counting S as a word."

"Sure." I didn't even count her words anymore. *"¿Qué deseas?"* I asked Margot.

Then Margot said in perfect English, "I think I'll have the Billion Dollar Shake, because the Million Dollar Shake is nine hundred and ninety-nine million dollars less than that."

Not even a Spanish accent!

Payton and I stared at her, mouths agape.

The man behind the counter said, "One Billion Dollar. What else?"

Margot ordered, "One Paparazzi, a S'more, and—" She turned to me. "What are you having?"

"You speak English!" Payton practically yelled at Margot.

"And Spanish. Both." She added, "Bilingual."

The worker said, "Yoo-hoo! What else?"

I ordered and we slid down the counter out of the way of the next customers. "Why did you let us believe you didn't speak English?" I asked.

"Billion Dollar!" the man slid Margot's shake down the counter.

"You assumed that." Margot stuck a straw in and sipped hard. "Then I just didn't tell you because I wanted to hear more about the lost treasure."

"You heard that?" My heart literally went THUD. I think it stopped for a sec. A quick glace around Millions of Milkshakes told me there was no portable defibrillator.

"So, were you pretending to not speak English or to be listening to your headphones?" Payton accused.

"Both, I guess."

"That's just wrong," Payton said. "Our conversations were private."

"You can be mad at me, or let me help," she said. "You know when money is scrunched up in a damp place it gets moldy and disintegrates. It could be getting eaten by worms right now. Or a rat is nibbling off little pieces to make a nest."

Payton said, "It's a family matter," as though she was part of the family.

"I know this city pretty well. I'm cruising around it all day in the sidecar of a Burrito Taxi," Margot said. "Plus I am kind of great at avoiding hazardous situations. I can steer you away from anything potentially dangerous."

"Like what?" I asked.

She started ticking off on her fingers. "Fire, hurricanes, coyotes, velociraptors, avalanches, hang gliding accidents, heat stroke . . . Want me to continue?"

Hello, weird, you've followed me to Hollywood.

"I think we get the idea," I said.

"She probably drives past *D* places all the time," Payton said to me. "And I hadn't even thought of the possibility of an avalanche."

"Oh, come on. I have *got* to do more on my spring break than drive in a sidecar." She used both thumbs to point to herself. "This girl needs a little fun."

"We *are* fun people," Payton said to me.

"It's a curse, I guess."

"I know. Right?"

I said, "It doesn't seem fair for her to miss out on fun during her break."

"And," Margot added, "I can make sure you always have a variety of burritos at your fingertips."

That did it!

"You're in!" Payton and I said.

"Looks like you had an exciting outing," Leo said when he saw our smiling faces, indented at the cheeks as we struggled to suck the thick shakes through the straws.

Margot said to him, "I might spend some time with the girls this week, Uncle Leo. They kinda need me to show them around the city. Is that okay?"

"I think it's a great idea," Leo said. "I mean, I'll miss you, of course, but I'll have me, myself, and I to keep me company."

I gave Leo his shake and called, "One-two-three-shoot!" and Payton and I each put out a rock, paper, or scissors with our hands.

I put out scissors, my fingers in a V.

Payton put out paper, a flat palm.

"Scissors cuts paper," I said. "You're in the back."

"Ugh."

"Don't worry. I'll hold your shake."

"Oh. Gee. Thanks."

Leo stopped in front of the Chinese Theatre, which was the epicenter of Hollywood tourism. It looked like a traditional Chinese palace theater, painted a royal red with temple bells, pagodas, and statues decorating the outside.

"Sorry it's so crowded. Lots of tour buses stop here," Leo said to me.

I sipped my shake—Justin Mania (Snickers and banana). "That's okay." Then I sipped the S'more shake.

"Hey!" Payton said. "Was that mine?"

"Nope," I lied.

Leo clipped a walkie onto my shorts. It weighed about ten pounds. "Let me know when you want me to pick you up." He handed Margot a fistful of business cards. "And I can make deliveries at the same time, so if anyone wants to place an order, just text it in."

"You sure you can handle this?" Margot asked him. "Don't drive while you're taking orders."

"I'll be fine," I said. "You show them the stars, the lights, the sights."

Payton was still unfolding herself from the backseat when I took another sip of the S'more. "Mmmm."

"That was definitely from mine," she guessed.

"Uh-uh," I lied again.

It took Payton a second to straighten up. She snatched the cup. "Gimme that." She felt its weight. "You totally had some."

"Oh, don't be a baby. We'll go back again later," I said. "Come on."

We pushed through the crowd in the forecourt of the movie theater, which was framed by high walls and home to lotus-shaped fountains. A group of girls wearing familiar-colored green skirts, sashes, and beanies gathered around a woman holding a Girl Scouts of America flag.

The leader pointed up. "Notice the dragon carved in stone. And those Heaven Dogs that guard the theater entrance were brought here from China. This theater was named Grauman's Chinese Theatre and then Mann's, and now TCL. It's not usual for historic sites to change names over time. This is the home of many spectacular premieres. Now look down. You'll see celebrities have imprinted their hands and feet in the courtyard's cement for decades. People travel from all over the world—"

Payton tugged the sleeve of my T. "Stay focused," she said. "You can read all about this later, if you're curious."

"Right. Focus," I said. "Wax museum."

"Is that where the money is hidden?" Margot asked without even a hint of lowering her voice.

Two boys looked at us. One of them asked, "Where is there money hidden?"

Payton gently pulled Margot away from them and explained, "She's new to English. She meant, 'Is that where the wax figures are on display?'"

We quickly moved away from them and navigated the sea of tourists until we saw Spider-Man standing at the entrance. He was surrounded by people taking pictures with him; of course, we had to do the same.

"How about if we start with the superhero section?" She led us into the museum to Hulk, Batman, Thor, then Robert Downey Jr. as Tony Stark.

"Wow, he looks so real," Payton said about Robert Downey.

"Very," I said.

Margot asked, "Explain to me what superheroes have to do with hidden mone—"

Payton stepped on her foot, which was bare except for a flimsy sandal.

Margot crunched in her lips to hold in a whimper. "You-know-who. Can I say that? I mean, that even worked for Harry Potter and Voldemort."

"You just said the name of He-Who-Must-Not-Be-Named," I pointed out.

"I was only trying to make a point. I won't say anything about the hidden money." She slapped a hand over her mouth and stepped away from Payton to protect her toes. "Sorry," Margot said. "That was the last time, I swear."

"Okay," I said. Then to Payton I said, "I don't think superheroes are ABJ's thing, but let's check out this Downey Jr. dude." We carefully roamed around the figure. I swear Tony Stark's eyes followed our every move.

"I'm not a fan of Iron Man," Margot said. "When he flies, he leaves emissions in the atmosphere and that can't be good for birds' lungs. It probably causes birdie birth defects."

"But he saves mankind," Payton said.

"And the world," I said.

"At the expense of the birds being able to breathe. Maybe you're okay with that kind of thing," Margot said.

"You know Iron Man isn't real?" Payton said.

"Duh. Right. If he was, I'd get the World Wildlife Federation to boycott him or something."

"Sure." I didn't know what else to say. I swear I must have a weird magnet. There is no other way to explain the statistical improbability that I could have this many weird people in my life.

Payton changed the subject, thankfully. "I don't know, I think ABJ is more into the old age of Hollywood stuff."

"Totally. Where's Dorothy?" I asked.

Margot spread her arms and let a brochure drape between them. She looked at an index and map, looked up, turned to face a different way, then back down at the brochure.

"You look like a tourist." Payton took the brochure, folded it back up, and tossed it into a nearby trash can. "That way." She pointed down a hall.

"How do you know that?" I asked.

"I don't," Payton said. "I just think we'll go this way, and if it's not there, we'll go the other way."

"Maps are very important," Margot said. "They help people from getting lost. Dangerous things happen to people when they're lost. I would never throw away—"

Payton stopped listening to Margot and hustled down a hall.

"She looks like she knows where she's going," I said to Margot. "Come on."

Payton led us to a gallery where round platforms displayed wax figures. This hall featured cinema classics. I probably know more of these characters than the average thirteen-year-old, because this is the kind of stuff my mom is into.

"I think this is the place," I said. There was Clint Eastwood, Greta Garbo, Lucille Ball, and Marilyn Monroe herself. "She really is beautiful." Every one of her wax features was perfect (hair, skin, eyes, dress), not unlike ABJ. I remembered that Marilyn died very young. "I wonder what she would be doing now if she was still alive?"

"Do you mean would she still be famous?" asked Payton.

"Yeah. ABJ reminds me of her. Somehow ABJ's fame faded. Would that have happened to Marilyn?"

"Maybe she would've played parts of older women, like moms and then grandmas?" Payton asked.

I'd seen Marilyn Monroe films, and I couldn't imagine her as a grandma.

"Or maybe when actresses get old they move to an island and retire," Payton said.

"Or," I looked at my pink sneakers, "maybe they lock themselves in their huge Hollywood home with their house-keeper as their only friend and wait for the phone to ring with a new script."

Payton tilted her head; she knew what I meant. But rather than let my thought go any further she said, "Let's find Dorothy."

On our way down another hall, Margot said, "I can't imagine why anyone would want to live on an island. I mean with the mosquitos, tsunamis, and sand sharks . . . No, thank you."

I looked at Payton out of the corner of my eye. If telepathy was possible, she would've heard me say, *Weird, right?*

We didn't talk anymore until we saw a blue-and-white gingham plaid dress ahead. I'd seen *The Wizard of Oz* a hundred times—okay, only fifty times all the way through, because the first fifty I stopped when the witch arrived—too scary.

There was a red velvet rope that protected Dorothy from people like me. Maybe not people exactly like me, because I doubted that the average tourist was searching for hidden money.

I jumped when Payton shouted, "Picnic basket!"

It was the perfect great place to hide money. *Who would look there?*

Margot asked, "You think there's . . . umm . . . you-know-what hiding in wax Dorothy's wax basket?"

Payton nodded and looked around at the crowd of people. "It's a risky place to store you-know-what."

"She could have stashed it here when she wasn't thinking clearly," I said. "Or maybe it was temporary, and then she forgot about it."

Margot asked, "Who are we talking about?"

"Ginger's aunt Betty-Jean," Payton explained. "Maybe Leo didn't tell you, but she's been acting strange, really forgetful. That's why she doesn't remember where she hid her stuff. But then this morning she seemed totally fine. Don't you think?"

"Yeah. But last night? That was super strange. I hope Mom can get some answers from the doctor today." I added, "But this does seem like a really non-secure place to hide money."

Payton said, "Let's look inside the basket."

That sounded like it should be easy, except for the rope between us and Dorothy. I could slip under it and peek inside her basket, but there were people around.

What do I do if I discover it's stuffed with cash? How would the people react when they saw it? "How am I going to do this?" I asked.

"You need a diversion," Margot said. "So no one is looking at you."

"You have any ideas?" I asked.

Payton curled her mouth to one side, then the other. That's what she does when she's thinking. "I do."

11

“You need to be fast, Ginger. If this works, it won’t be for long.” Payton walked to the other side of the room and clapped her hands. “Excuse me, wax museum peeps.”

The crowd looked at her.

“I’m Payton Paterson.” She pointed to a name tag that she wasn’t even wearing. “Future owner of Dr. Paterson’s and Dr. Carlson’s Transplant Institute. But today, I’m working undercover with the Association of Paranormal Activities.”

“You’re like a real ghostbuster?” a boy asked.

“Well, an intern actually. I mean, come on, I’m only thirteen, right? And we prefer the term Professional Phantom Patrol, or the PPP.” She continued, “I don’t want to alarm any of you, but there’s a sitch here at this museum, and I've been asked to clear out this room. You know, they give interns boring jobs."

Margot and I went to work.

We limboed under the rope . . . my heart jumped.

"A ghost? Is there a ghost here right now?" the same boy asked.

I reached for the basket with my sweaty hands . . . my heart jumped again.

"Um . . . We're picking up indicators of potential activity and need to perform some tests. It should only take about fifteen minutes." She pointed to the corridor opposite Dorothy. "You can head out this way, maybe check out the *Star Wars* collection, and then come back. I've heard the stormtroopers and Chewbacca are awesome." She totally got that from Grant. Payton had thought Chewbacca was a kind of gum. "It's for your own safety. Intern or not, I know these things can be unpredictable."

I tried to lift the basket lid . . . it wouldn't open.

I tried to get my hand under the lid . . . it wouldn't budge.

People asked Payton questions as they progressed to the hallway she'd indicated.

"As an intern, I only have Level One clearance, so I don't have all the answers, but if it was nothing, would they have asked me to clear this gallery? Probably not, right?"

No hinge.

No place to put money.

The basket was a wax prop through and through.

I made an exaggerated frown face in Payton's direction.

She picked up her cell phone. "Hello." She paused. "Wait, peeps! Two words: false alarm. The readings have returned to normal. You can come back in." She added, "The PPP thanks you for your cooperation."

She came over to Dorothy. "Nothing?"

"It wouldn't even open."

"Bummer," she said.

Margot said, "I can't believe all those people were going to leave."

"Seems there's a natural curiosity about ghosts," I said. "It sure did come in handy."

"I know. Right?" Payton lifted her knee, and with an exaggerated tilt of her head pointed me to it.

I lifted my knee and we tapped them together—knee high-five.

"What was that?" Margot asked.

Payton said, "You ask too many questions. Just pick up your knee and tap it to ours."

Payton and I lifted our knees again to meet Margot's. She smiled, but she didn't seem to know what she was smiling about.

Then Payton asked, "What else should we hit while we're here?"

"Maybe we should ask ABJ?" I removed the oversize walkie-talkie from my purse that I'd hung across my chest. The walkie was so big and heavy that my purse strap dug into my neck leaving a groove I could feel with my fingers. "Why didn't I think of this sooner?" I pushed the button. "ABJ, it's Ginger here."

Grant's voice came on. "Don't even ask me to beam you up, because I won't. I'll let you float around in a zero-gravity environment until your O_2 runs out."

"Is that your brother?" Margot asked. "Tell him we're not in a zero-gravity blah-blah-blah." Then she added, "I have an older brother who is all sports, all the time."

"*That*," I said, "sounds normal."

"*That*," Payton pointed to the walkie to indicate Grant, "isn't."

I told Grant, "Just give the walkie to ABJ."

There was a moment of static. "Hello, Gingersnap."

"If you hid the money near or around a wax person whose name started with a *D*, who would it be?"

"Hmmm. Let me think. Maybe Sammy Davis Jr.? Ummm . . . that's the only person I can think of right now."

I said, "Okay. We'll check it out. I felt good about Dorothy, but I can't open her basket."

"That was a good guess. I like her. I'd trust her wax look-alike to guard my money. Try Sammy. I gotta get back to this *Star Trek* marathon that your brother has me watching." Then she added, "Over and out." I bet Leo had taught her that.

Grant's voice came back on. "Get me wax."

I turned the walkie off.

"Sammy, huh?" Payton started wandering.

Margot picked up a crinkled brochure off a ledge and skimmed her finger down the list of attractions in the brochure. "She's not here."

"Sammy is a *he*," I said.

"Oh. Well, *he*'s not here."

Payton said, "I'm ready for a snack, and since *someone* drank half of my shake, I want another one."

"I could go for another myself," I said. "But first I have to stop at the gift shop for something for the space spaz."

On our way I asked Margot, "Have you ever tried to eat only ice cream all day?"

"No," she said. "Is that a thing?"

"It could be," Payton said.

Margot said, "Why would anyone do that? You'd miss out on the daily recommended amount of so many vitamins."

"True," Payton agreed, but I knew for certain that Payton didn't agree at all. She wanted to try to eat nothing but milkshakes all day.

I bought a wax Darth Vader for Grant, and called Leo on the walkie. "Hey, it's us. Can you bring us back to Millions of Milkshakes?"

"Yup. *Oui. Sí.* Going for two-in-one-day? That's smart. I'll pick you up at Walt Disney's star." Then he said, "Over." The walkie went to static.

Payton looked up. "Star?"

12

Margot pointed to the sidewalk—shiny black squares with gold flecks. "Stars," she said. Then she pointed up and down Hollywood Boulevard at the Walk of Fame, which had brass stars embedded in the sidewalk. "Lots of stars. Each one is like a monument to someone in entertainment."

"Of course," I said. "That's on our list."

"Disney. *D*," Payton suggested.

"Yeah." I looked up and down the street again. "There are tons of them."

"Statistically, a lot would be *D*," Payton said.

"We have a little time," I said. "Let's ask ABJ her fave. It's worth a try." I pushed the button of the walkie. "Ginger here. Come in, ABJ."

Margot asked, "You guys like the letter *D*, huh?"

I would have to explain the D clue to Margot later. For now I nodded as my mom came on the walkie. "Ginger, is that you?" Then I could hear her talking to someone else. "It's Ginger and Payton. I wonder where they are."

"Mom," I said, but she couldn't hear me because she didn't take her finger off the button. I could still hear voices in the background.

"Ginger, can you hear me?" And she said to someone, "I don't think we have a good connection."

The line was static for a hot second and I was able to say, "Lemme talk to ABJ."

"Ginger?" ABJ asked.

"We're at the Walk of Fame doing you-know-what. Do you have a favorite brass star?"

"I have a brass lamp," she said.

Huh?

"We're working on the . . . the mission. You know, looking for something," I said.

"I would look for you to the edge of the Earth, Cassidy." She recited a line from her award-winning movie. "And I'd comb the bottom of the deepest oceans."

"Ginger, it's Dad. I think ABJ is getting tired. We'll

just see you when you get back, okay? Leo said he's picking you up."

"Is she okay?" I asked.

"She's gonna take a nap and then we're going to the doctor. Over."

I clicked the walkie off slowly and kept my eyes on the ground.

"The doctor will be able to explain it," Payton said.

"I hope so."

"I love that movie, *The Edge of the Earth*. Except for the part when Cassidy runs barefoot on the boardwalk. I mean, has she ever heard of a splinter? You get one of those and neglect it, and you're looking at possible amputation," Margot said. "But it's no surprise she won an award for that movie."

I telepathically said to Payton, *Seriously? Amputation? All this girl thinks about is doom and gloom.*

"Yeah," I said. "It's a great movie. We have to get that award back for her."

"Her Oscar? Are you kidding me?! It's with the hidden money?!" Margot exclaimed.

Payton stretched her foot over to Margot's exposed toes and stepped down.

"Ow! That's it!" Margot said. "I'm buying sneakers!"

"Or, you can turn on your filter and stop saying that out loud," Payton suggested.

"Come on, you two," I said, but Payton was right, Margot had no filter. "Let's start with Sammy Davis Jr.'s star. He was her first pick last time."

Margot grabbed the map that she had in her back pocket.

"Jeez," Payton said, "so embarrassing. Only tourists use maps." She took a step away from us.

I glanced around the crowds of people. "Everyone here is a tourist. We're blending in."

Payton looked around and seemed to maybe agree that maybe we didn't look as dorky as she felt.

Margot said, "Sammy is a few blocks that way," and started in that direction.

"How would ABJ hide you-know-what and you-know-what, the second you-know-what is the Oscar, near or around one of these stars?" Margot asked.

I said, "If you're going to tell us what you-know-what is, it's kind of unnecessary to call it you-know-what."

"True," Margot said. "But I mean the stars are *in* the cement."

"I don't know. Maybe she put the goods under it?" Payton suggested.

"How would we check? We don't have a crowbar or jackhammer—wait—do one of you have a crowbar or jackhammer?" Margot asked.

Payton and I held up our arms showing that we weren't carrying any power tools.

I only had my little purse around my wrist, which couldn't fit anything besides the ten-pound walkie-talkie and the little plastic bag with Grant's wax gift.

Margot said, "Right. Of course you don't. If you did, that would practically scream, 'We're searching for hidden money and an Oscar on Hollywood Boulevard!'"

Told ya—no filter.

13

I said, "Let's get to Sammy and Walt."

"Then shakes," Payton added.

"Totally. Where did Margot go?" I asked.

"Maybe following a map to a jackhammer."

"Ha!" I said, "Do you think she has a thin cerebral cortex?"

"Or maybe she processes language in her less-dominant brain hemisphere, and lacks the neurons to process thoughts before her mouth makes sounds."

"Good theory," I said. "In either event, she has no control over what comes out of her mouth."

"Totally," Payton agreed.

"But I like her," I said.

"I do too, but have you noticed that she sees the worst possible things in everything?" Payton asked again.

"How could I not notice? She's talking about velociraptors."

Payton found Sammy Davis Jr.'s star before we found Margot.

"Should we worry about her?" I asked.

She looked at her watch. "Let's wait ten minutes before we worry. She knew we were coming here and she has a map."

"I just hope she doesn't get a splinter."

We laughed.

"Take my picture." I handed Payton my phone and crouched down by Sammy's brass star. I ran my hand around every crevice. I don't know what I expected to happen. Maybe it could've opened up like the hatch of a submarine and under it would be a pile of cash and an Oscar. Payton and I would casually pick it up and walk away and nobody would even look at us twice, right?

Payton said, "Look up and smile."

I looked up without smiling. CLICK—swoop—it went to QuickPik. "I was kidding about the picture. I just want to look normal while I'm down here massaging Sammy's star." None of the letters on the star opened a secret door á la

Scooby Doo. "Margot was right. We need a crowbar to look under this." I glanced around the sidewalk. "I don't think this is right. I don't think ABJ could hide money here."

"Me either. We need to think of something else. A shake will fuel our brains. You know, omega-three oils," Payton said.

"That's in fish."

"Well, I'm not eating a fish smoothie. Blech!" Payton stuck out her tongue. "I'm sure ice cream has something that stimulates brain waves."

She was probably right. "Where's Disney? And where is Margot?" I looked up and down the street, but didn't see her yet. "Now I'm starting to worry."

Payton picked up an index of the stars and handed it to me. "See if you can find Walt."

"Why can't you?"

"I don't want to look like a tourist," she said. And then, like a total tourist, she CLICK—*swoop*—sent a picture of Hollywood Boulevard to QuickPik.

I checked out the index. "Oops. Problem."

"What kind?"

"Walt has two stars," I said. "Ha! And Mickey Mouse has one too."

"Not Minnie? That's not fair."

"Well, Snow White has one, so it sounds like it's an equal opportunity Walk of Fame."

"That's good to know," Payton said. "How far are we from Walt's first star?"

Margot said from behind us, "Uncle Leo meant the one that's up there, on the other side of the street."

"Where were you?" I asked. "I was nervous."

She held up a foot. She was wearing pink sneakers, just like Payton's and mine. "Like 'em?"

"Love 'em!" I said.

"Good find!" Payton agreed.

We didn't walk far before we saw a burrito/banana was pulled over. Leo handed out foil-wrapped packages to anyone waving a five-dollar bill.

Just as we arrived he said, "Sorry, folks. Sold out. But text me an order and I'll deliver it." He tossed burrito-shaped business cards into the group of gatherers, who shoved to get one.

Someone said something that I didn't hear, and Leo said, "This just isn't your lucky day. I already have passengers." He looked our way. "And here they are now." He opened the taxi door like a fancy chauffeur. "Lovely to see you, ladies."

"Hey, Leo!" we said.

I paused for Payton to get in.

"Uh-huh," she said and put her hand behind her back. "One-two-three shoot!"

I put out scissors.

Payton put out rock.

Rock smashes scissors.

"Ugh." I climbed in the back.

Leo said to Margot, "I dig your new kicks."

14

"Coming through." Leo entered ABJ's house with his arms full of steaming burritos fresh out of the trunk. "Dinner's here!"

"Hot stuff!" he called.

"Lay it on me," Dad said.

Leo delivered one per person.

ABJ took hers, but just set it on her lap. I noticed there was no burrito sparkle in her eyes as we dug into our foil treats.

Margot sat between Payton and me at the dining room table. "Mmm," we all hummed in unison.

"Pork this time," Payton said.

"Good call," I said.

"Just the right amount of cilantro," Payton said.

I asked, "Did I just taste pineapple?"

"You did," Margot said.

Leo puffed his chest out and soaked up the compliments.

"My people would like this." Grant didn't even attempt to close his mouth when he chewed. *What is it with boys?* We were used to Grant making comments like this, so no one usually commented about stuff like his "people," but Margot didn't really know Grant.

She asked, "You think you're an alien?"

"I don't *think* I'm an alien."

"Oh. You mean you *are* an alien?"

He smiled.

"From what planet? Were you sent here to collect soil samples? Or to study humankind or the Earth's resources? I've heard that most planets are anxious to get their hands on cactus. Who would have thought that cacti would be the thing that would start an interplanetary war?"

"Um . . . errr." Grant had never had anyone ask him serious questions about his true heredity.

We all just looked at him, because these were good questions, and I think we were all curious about the answers.

"You look kind of like your dad. Isn't that a coincidence if he's not really your father?"

"Umm . . . err."

I enjoyed seeing Grant squirm through Margot's inquisition.

She added, "Oh, they probably made your Earth body look like that so no one would suspect. I guess that's smart, actually. So this isn't what you look like when you're at home? How long will you be here?"

Grant said, "I'm not at liberty to talk about my mission."

"Sure." Margot took a big bite of burrito. "I get that. That's cool."

Leo prompted a different line of questioning to Mom and Dad. "Bank update?"

"Accounts are empty," Dad said. "The one account where she kept the bulk of her money—the one the bank automatically deducted the mortgage payment from—was cleaned out about four months ago. ABJ went in and withdrew it all, in cash. They have the records."

"What did she do with it?" Leo asked.

Mom looked at ABJ, who still hadn't touched her burrito. "She doesn't know."

"I suspect it's gone. Spent," Dad said. "Or maybe even stolen."

"Or," Grant started, "she buried it. Like a pirate."

"Ha, ha!" I said.

Payton added, "You are cute, Grant. Very cute."

"So cute," I supported her. "Next you'll be saying it was snatched by aliens."

"That would be funny," Payton said.

"I know. Right?" I added.

"Two words—funny kid."

"Yeah," Margot said. "Imagine hiding all your money and leaving a weird clue about where it was stashed." Then she exclaimed, "Ouch!" as Payton pressed her weight onto Margot's toe. It sounded like it hurt even through sneakers.

"What's the matter?" Leo asked.

Margot said, "Just a splinter."

"How did—"

Mom interrupted Leo, "Girls, don't joke about this situation. It isn't funny."

"It's not," Leo agreed. "But I hope none of that's true—that 'gone, spent, stolen,' or 'the pirate burial,' and definitely not the 'alien abduction.'"

"Uncle Leo." Margot looked at Payton and me for a second before continuing, "If any of that were true, do you think anyone would actually talk about it out loud? I mean, then just anyone could run around Hollywood, in and out of museums, and up and down the Walk of Fame, looking everywhere for a wad of cash and an Oscar."

"Who said anything about an Oscar?" Leo asked. "Is that missing too?"

We looked at each other.

I explained, "Just misplaced. Margot wanted to see it, and ABJ didn't remember where she had stored it."

"Probably the attic," Payton said. "That's where my family stores stuff."

Leo said, "That's probably it. We can check it out later. But I'd like to get to the bottom of this money thing, because the bank isn't going to be patient much longer about this house. And I want to use my back pay to invest in another taxi. You know, expand." Then he looked at ABJ's unopened foil. "Aren't you hungry, beautiful?"

"I think I'll lie down."

"Do you want help?" Mom asked.

"No thanks, honey." She pushed her chair back and walked behind me, and kissed the top of my head. "Good night, Ginger," she said. Then she whispered in my ear, "Things change over time." She reached down and secretly put something in my hand. I squeezed my finger around it, then she walked toward her bedroom.

"Good night, Aunt Betty-Jean," I called after her. When she was gone I asked, "What did the doctor say?"

Mom took a few papers from her purse and set them on the table. "He thinks it's the early stages of Alzheimer's disease. He gave her medicine to take every day to slow it down, but"—she glanced at the white tile floor—"there's no cure."

I read the top paper: HOW TO SLOW THE PROGRESSION OF ALZHEIMER'S DISEASE.

I had the very beginning of an idea, but no time to think about it right now. I stored the idea in the place in my brain where I file things that I want to think about later. It doesn't have a scientific name, but it's in my limbic system. I think of it my *mentalus storageum*.

Dad continued, "The doctor said that it's not unusual for people to think clearly in the morning, and then have trouble later in the day."

Mom said, "Maybe we can adjust her schedule to accommodate for that. You know, plan her activities and visits in the morning."

"She doesn't have any activities," Leo said. "She doesn't visit or get visitors. Besides me, that is."

Everyone was quiet as we started to better understand ABJ's life. It was different from the life I'd imagined. No premieres, no big Hollywood parties, no celebrity friends. I guess some actresses got parts as grandmothers, some retired to Caribbean islands, and some hung out all day in their Hollywood homes, dressed up for guests or journalists or fans who would never come. Some had only one friend, her housekeeper, when he wasn't running a Burrito Taxi business. And, was he really a *friend*? Or was he an *employee*?

Admiring the lights of the Hollywood valley below, I thought that even this fancy Hollywood home with all its glam, sculptures, and mirrors, was really a cave, and ABJ was trapped in it.

I took the doctor papers from the table to read more carefully. I wasn't ready to accept that there was nothing we could do for her.

Later, as I walked upstairs to bed, I finally opened my hand and looked down to see what ABJ gave me. A matchbook.

15

I woke up to Payton's face an inch away from mine. "Yikes! What the heck, Payt?"

"I'm freaking out!" she said. "It might be a panic attack."

"Chill. We're gonna search more today. We'll find the money and award, pay Leo so he can get a second burrito car, and pay the mortgage to keep ABJ in this house"—*and out of my Delaware bedroom*—"and maybe get her a nurse," I said. "I thought we could go to the Dolby today."

"Dolby, dandy," she said. "But the Olympics." She pointed to the countdown app. It read: NINETY-SIX HOURS. "We need a schedule, Ginger. A schedule!"

"I like schedules."

"Do I need to remind you about the DeMarcos?" She

planted a hand on her hip and I noticed that she was completely dressed, pink sneakers and all.

"No. You don't have to remind me. I know the DeMarcos very well. How long have you been awake?"

"Long time, Ginger. A long time," she said. "And I made a pot of coffee. Want some?"

Not if it makes me like you. "No thanks."

"So how about the schedule?" Payton read from a yellow legal pad. "We could wake up early, starting today, and make the molds and do the crafty stuff. Then at night we can sand the molds and do the labels."

"I like it." *Do I have a choice? I am actually a little afraid of you right now.* "But how early are we talking?"

She looked at the time on her phone. "Like five."

"Payton," I said. "Is it five a.m. now?"

"On the button."

"Ugh." I pulled the pillow over my face.

She yanked it off. "It's the *Olympics* were talking about! If we were Olympic figure skaters, we'd be in the rink right now. This is no different."

I didn't comment on her analogy, which wasn't too bad, even though it meant I had to get out of bed.

• • •

We worked on the patio so that we could talk without worrying that we would wake anyone up. After a while, and I'm not even sure how long it was because once we got into science mode, time seemed to disappear, Payton said, "I smell croissant."

Sure enough ABJ pulled open the French doors and walked out holding a crystal tray with three croissants on doilies. She looked like she was hiding a hair salon and makeup artist in her bedroom. Today her house robe was pale blue and edged with a puffy boa. It brought out the color of her eyes.

"Good morning, girls." She took a nibble of a croissant and called over her shoulder, "They're perfect, Leo!" To us she said, "A man who can make a burrito and a croissant! If only he was twenty years older—wait, even better—if I was twenty years *younger*, I'd snatch him up." Her smile showed off her beautiful white teeth.

I imagined that if Marilyn Monroe were still alive, she would look like this—elegant, radiant, stylish . . . At least until the afternoon, when she became someone else, who was equally as beautiful, but couldn't think straight.

Leo set a cappuccino down next to ABJ. His hair darted in all directions. If ABJ was twenty years younger, they would be the most opposite couple *ever*. She was sophisticated, and he smelled like yesterday's pork.

"Where's Margot?" I asked.

"She's organizing our day. Making a chart or something. That sidecar is like her little office. She'll come in soon." He went back into the kitchen.

"Tell me what you have here." Her manicured hand indicated the model we'd worked on.

"This is our project for the Science Olympics," I said proudly.

"It's not done yet, of course," Payton said.

"We're going to sculpt the shape and sections of an actual brain," I added.

"And then make labels—"

"That we'll glue to toothpicks—"

"And stick them in the right places—"

ABJ interrupted, "I get it."

She nibbled another piece of her croissant and studied the mold. She tilted her head. "Hmmm . . ."

"What?"

"I like it fine, but these cats, the DeMarcos, are making a robot, you say?"

"Yup. We're gonna kick their butts," I said.

"Is this robot going to move around and do stuff?" she asked.

"I'm sure," Payton said. "The DeMarcos are serious about their science."

"Hmmm." She studied the mold some more.

"What is it?" Payton asked.

"You don't like it?" I asked.

"No, I do. I can see it's going to be a lovely model of the brain complete with toothpick flags." Then she added, "I just wonder . . ."

"What?" Payton asked.

"Wonder what?" I asked.

"When I audition for parts, I always think about how I can stand out." She picked a tiny spoon off the saucer and stirred the foam and coffee together with *clink clink* against the side of the cappuccino cup. "So I'm wondering what about this will stand out among a crowd of Olympians?"

I looked at the white round ball of clay. In my mind I could see every crack and crevice of the brain carved and molded, every toothpick a different color, every flag typed— maybe even laminated—with meticulously researched details about the brain parts. It would be perfect. It would totally win. *Right?*

Leo returned to the patio with three bowls of pineapple.

"For you." He gave a bowl to ABJ. "And for my new friends." He gave one to Payton and to me.

ABJ poked a fork into a chunk and held it up. "Leo's business stands out," she said. "The taxi, the taste, the business cards . . . all of it."

"Thanks," he said. "You have to think of ways to make your product va-voom, kapow, *ooh la la.*"

I considered the brain model again. *Ooh la la?* Just because it was perfect (which it would be), would it *kapow?*

16

Leo dropped Payton, Margot, and me off at the Walk of Fame near the Dolby Theatre in time for us to get tickets to the ten-thirty tour. I looked off into the distance, where I could make out the Hollywood sign in the smog. (Apparently, even celebrities have to deal with bad air quality out here).

Entering the theater there were storefronts on either side of a grand staircase. Suddenly, the Dolby looked familiar to me. I'd seen it on TV during the annual Academy Awards show. I took a picture of the columns that displayed names of past award winners. *Mom would love this!* Maybe we should've invited her.

During the ceremony, the famous red carpet rested on

the path we'd just walked from the Burrito Taxi and extended all the way up the stairs. Film royalty arrived in limos and entered the Awards in the very spot we were standing on.

I pretended to hold a microphone. "How does it feel to be nominated tonight?" I asked Payton.

"It's like a dream come true. I am just so thankful to the Academy."

"Do you think you'll win?"

"It's a thrill to even be nominated." Then she pretended to wave to someone in the distance.

"Who are you waving to?" Margot asked.

"Oh," Payton said. "There's Nick Jonas. I have to thank him for the birthday card. Please excuse me."

"What?" Margot looked to where Payton was indicating. "There's no one there."

I explained, "She was pretending."

"Right," Margot said. "Of course. I mean, could you imagine if Nick Jonas was there? And if he'd sent you a birthday card?"

Then my mind tingled for a sec, like it does when I think deep science-y thoughts. "I wonder if ABJ can still imagine things, you know, when her mind is in 'another place'?" I wasn't looking for an answer.

"What do you think she meant by 'Things change over time'?" Payton asked. I'd told Payton and Margot what ABJ whispered.

"I don't know. Maybe she was sort of talking in her sleep, but awake," I said.

Payton twirled a bit of hair and said, "huh," like she does when she's contemplating a theory. "Maybe. I wonder if that could happen."

"Maybe," Margot repeated. "You know what I wonder? I wonder if we could build chutes, like the kind at a bank drive-through, around the city, and people could stick their burrito order in the chute and then we could shoot a burrito back to them. That way we could get food to people two different ways—taxi delivery and chute." She paused. "Wait. What am I thinking? Bacteria would grow in the chutes and larvae would grow and customers would get sick and we would get sued and lose the taxi. Forget it."

I often thought that my mind and Payton's were unlike that of other girls our age, because we really think about and discuss science-y possibilities. But maybe we weren't as unique as I'd thought. Margot's hypothalamus seemed equally overactive, only it focused on anything that could possibly go wrong with anything.

A voice bellowed from the Dolby Theatre's overhead sound system. "If you have a ticket for the ten-thirty a.m. tour, please convene at the theater entrance."

That's us!

Our tour guide introduced himself as Harry. And he was unique.

Harry had a bit of an issue in the pants department. He wore them about as high as they could go, and kept them there by tightening his belt—really snug—around his lumpy belly.

"My lord," Margot said to him. "Does that hurt?"

Payton subtly put her foot on top of Margot's pink sneaker and shifted her weight down onto Margot's foot.

"What? What did I do now? I didn't even mention the money."

Payton and I rolled our eyes. It seemed like Margot really couldn't control what came out of her mouth. In a way, ABJ and Margot had a similar condition—neither could control when her brain was malfunctioning.

Harry either didn't hear, or didn't care, or didn't know what Margot was talking about, because he started his introduction. "The Academy Awards is an annual event when the film industry recognizes the winners of the prestigious Oscars." He tugged at his self-inflicted wedgie. There had to be something Dad could invent to help people who want to wear their pants up high but not get wedgies. I tucked that away in my *mentalus storageum*. I'd tell Dad later. "Winners are given a gold-plated statue of a knight standing on a reel of film."

He continued, "An Oscar is eight and a half pounds and thirteen and a half inches high. Winners must agree to give the Academy a first right of refusal to buy back the Oscar if it is ever no longer wanted. This is to prevent the private buying or selling of the statuettes, which is illegal."

"Wouldn't it be funny if she hid her Oscar here, at the home of the Oscars?" Payton whispered.

"Ironic, I guess," I said.

Margot whispered, "Can I talk about you-know-what if I whisper?"

I put a "shh" finger in front of my lips.

Inside, the main auditorium was glitzy; the thirty-three hundred seats were red velvet.

"I need another diversion."

Margot asked me, "What are you gonna do?"

I cringed when I thought of my plan. "It's dirty."

Payton smooshed up her nose. "Then don't tell us."

I asked Payton, "Can you get everyone to look somewhere other than down there at those seats?"

"I think I can. Let's see . . . Should I fall? Faint? Puke? . . . Oh, I've got it!" Payton pushed me away to get started. "This is going to be a good one." She said to Margot, "Just go with it, okay?"

"I can do that," Margot said.

Before we left ABJ's house, I'd checked out the seating chart of the Dolby online. I was ready to dash to each of the theater's seating sections and examine row *D*. Actually, I planned to look *under* row *D* because that's someplace you could *look, but not see.*

"Oh my God!" Payton screeched and pointed to a private red-velvet-lined box where VIPs would sit above the heads of the main audience.

Harry stopped his speech to inform Payton of the tour rules. "Please raise your hand if you have a question or comment." He hiked his pants up to a level that didn't seem possible and must have been painfully uncomfortable.

"But did you see that?" Payton asked the tour group.

Harry said, "Raising your hand means everyone will get to say what they want and no one will walk on each other's words."

No one listened to him.

"You mean over there?" Margot asked Payton and pointed.

All eyes moved where indicated.

Payton threw her hand in the air, but didn't wait for Harry to call on her. "Is this place haunted? Because I clearly saw a ghost there." She pointed up.

Once all eyes were up, I dashed. I couldn't see the rest of the diversion, but I heard all. "There have been rumors."

An older lady asked, "Who was it, sweetie?"

Her little old lady friend asked, "Where?"

Payton said, "The private box. Up there." Everyone looked. "Oh my gosh. I just got a chill. There is definitely a phantasm of some kind in here. Can you feel it?" she asked. "I just finished an internship with the APA—Association of Paranormal Activity—and I saw many a ghost. Many. So, I know what one looks like and I'm telling you, there was one up there."

"I see it!" Margot exclaimed.

"Who was it?" asked the first lady.

"Hard to tell, since he was translucent," Payton explained.

"He was?" Harry asked.

"He totally was."

Payton was doing great. This ghost thing was golden!

"Then how do you know it was a man?" the lady asked.

Payton said, "Just a feeling. It might have been uh . . . uh . . . Sammy Davis Jr."

"Did you see his glass eye?" Harry asked.

"Yes! Eeeeexactly. His glass eye. That's what I saw."

"Wait." Harry paused. "Do you hear that?"

By now I was on my back scooting down row *D* of the mezzanine section. I clicked on the flashlight I'd strapped to my head—another of Dad's inventions. Headlamps have been around, but remote-controlled headlights were a whole new and emerging market. I could shift the light in any direction with a little move of my thumb.

I wasn't sure what I was looking for, maybe storage pouches on the bottoms of the chairs, or maybe a map to lead us to the real treasure. I looked and felt for everything.

"I hear it," Margot said.

"What do you hear?" Payton asked.

"It sounds like—" Margot paused.

"Like tapping. Like he's tap-dancing in the afterlife."

"That's what I was going to say," Margot said.

"I just got a chill," one of the little old ladies said.

"Have you ever had a paranormal investigator here?" Payton asked. "You know, ghost hunters?"

Harry stuttered, "Umm . . . I . . . umm . . . I don't know."

"Because I have connections with the PPP."

Margot asked Payton, "Want me to get them on the phone?"

Harry asked, "What's PPP?"

"Professional Phantom Patrol," Payton said.

"I've never heard of them."

"Seriously?" Margot gawked. "Dude, you gotta get out of the Dolby sometimes."

Payton added, "There's a whole world out there."

This line of chatter continued for a while.

I'd prepared myself to be crawling in sticky, buttery, gummy muck, but this floor shined like ABJ's foyer. I guess the Academy Awards have certain standards for cleanliness. If there's one kind of standards I like, it's standards for cleanliness.

Payton said, "This place could be full of ghosts of stars just waiting for their names to be called to win their Oscar."

"That makes sense," Harry said. "And it's consistent with the rumors."

"I would imagine so. Is there someone you can call?" Payton asked.

"Like my manager?"

"That's a start," Payton said. "Then I can hook you and your management up with the PPP."

What is she saying?

The PPP is pretend!

"I just saw it!" the second old lady cried. "But it was a woman. Her gown shimmered in the light."

"I saw it too!" her friend exclaimed. "She was floating."

Jeez, Payton has these guys going.

I finished the *D* rows of mezzanine I and II. Now I had to get down to the orchestra section. I followed a lighted exit sign into the hallway, down a set of stairs, and prepared to repeat the process.

I looked up and saw Harry on the phone. "We seem to have a paranormal disturbance on the ten-thirty a.m. tour," he said to someone. Maybe his manager. He pulled up his pants with his free hand, then rested it on his silver belt buckle like it was a shelf.

Maybe suspenders would help Harry. Well, it would keep the pants up, but wouldn't help with the wedgie.

I got to work backstroking through all of the *D* rows. I only found a pack of Tic Tacs, $3.42 in coins, a button, and a bobby pin. Not what I'd hoped. I stood in the lowest level of the theater, turned off my headlight, and wiped my hands on my pants before squirting them with hand sanitizer that I kept in my pocket.

Then I propped my clean hands on my hips and studied the magnificent theater, considering where else something could be hidden. The VIP box seats made the most sense because they have more privacy. But both the boxes themselves and the rows therein were numbered, (I'd learned that online), so no D.

One of the ladies looked down at me and pointed. "Look! There's another one?"

She was pointing at *me*!

I had a few choices, I guess. I could float around and act ghostly or . . . well, I didn't know my other choices.

"Uh . . . were you entranced?" Payton asked me.

"Did you levitate down there?" Margot asked.

That sounded like a good explanation. "Yes. That must be what happened. I heard Sammy playing the trumpet and the next thing I know, I was floating down here."

The other old lady said, "Sammy Davis Jr. didn't play the trumpet."

Payton said, "As far as we know."

The first old lady added, "Maybe he always *wanted* to,

and now he's learning how in the afterlife."

"That's probably it," Payton said.

Harry hung up his cell. "On behalf of the Dolby Theatre and the Academy of Motion Picture Arts and Sciences, I have to cut this tour short due to spectral interference." To me he asked, "Do you need a doctor?"

"I think I'm okay."

To Payton, Harry said, "We're calling the PPP. Well, my manager is. Thanks for the recommendation."

"Good idea, Harry," Payton said. "Happy to help."

17

Back on Hollywood Boulevard I said to Payton, "That was impressive."

"Impressive and awesome!" Margot said. "You're like the fastest liar on Earth."

"It's not lying," Payton said. "It's *improvising*."

"Then you're like the fastest improviser ever," Margot said.

I asked, "You know that the PPP and APA aren't real?"

"I know. Right? I was so into it that I started believing it myself."

"Well, *that* performance deserves an award," I said.

"I have two words: milkshakes."

"I think that's one word," Margot said.

"You're right," I said. "It is." I didn't know if Margot would get the Payton-ism about miscounting words. "I don't know if the Academy would approve of a second milkshake."

"I'll make it a gold-plated flavor. They should be okay with that," Payton said.

"Good plan," I said, "but I'm not sure I have money." I reached in my pocket to see what I had. I had something, but it wasn't money.

"What's that?" Payton asked.

"It's something that ABJ secretly stuffed it into my hand last night." I held up the matchbook.

"It's from the Brown Derby," Margot read. "It's a restaurant."

"And a *D*," Payton said.

"It is," I said.

"And a *B*," Margot said. "Brown starts with a *B*."

"I have a good feeling about this. I think ABJ wants us to go there."

"Then let's do it," Payton said.

"I'm in," Margot said.

The address on the matchbook was 1628 Vine Street. I plugged it into my phone's GPS. "It's less than a mile away."

110

Margot looked at her sneakers. "I've got my walking shoes."

Payton looked past my shoulder behind me and gave a little gasp. She grabbed my arm and whispered, "You won't believe what I'm seeing."

"Sammy Davis Jr. tap-dancing with a glass eye and a trumpet? You're right. I won't believe that. Enough, Payt, let's go."

"It's Harry. He is talking to someone and pointing at us," Payton said.

"He looks mad," Margot said.

"Do you think he figured out that the Dolby isn't haunted?" I asked.

"Or maybe his manager did," Payton said. "He's walking this way."

"Let's get out of here," I said.

"We could speed walk." Margot bolted down the street swinging her arms and taking giant steps, like a professional speed walker.

Payton looked over her shoulder. "Um, they're crossing the street."

"If we get in trouble, my mom won't let us out around town anymore. So maybe we can run!" I suggested and zipped past Margot.

"That's not good for your joints," Margot called after me. "And you could get shin splints."

Despite her warning, we didn't stop, and after a few seconds, Margot started running too.

"I know how we can lose him for sure," I said. "Follow me."

Harry looked all around, but he couldn't see us and we were right in front of him. He crossed the street and went down an alley.

Once he was far enough away, we took the green beanies off our heads, removed the sashes, and returned them to two Girl Scouts. Then Payton and I each held up three fingers and said to the girls, "I will live by the Girl Scout Law."

"I don't know if I can make a pledge like that without first consulting with an attorney," Margot said.

"No one will pressure you to take an oath you're not comfortable with," I assured her.

"All those years of campfire songs came in handy." I headed in the direction of the Brown Derby, keeping a careful eye behind us.

"Totally," Payton agreed.

"Campfires? That sounds like an accident waiting to

happen," Margot said. "Things are dry out here in California. One small fire can get out of control and travel through a whole canyon."

The glasses in Margot's world all seemed to be half empty.

It didn't take more than a few minutes to find the building marked 1628, but it clearly was not the Brown Derby.

It was an apartment building.

"What the—" Payton said.

I checked the address on the matchbook. "This is definitely right."

"Is there another Vine Street?" I asked Margot.

"No. With all of the taxi navigation that I do, I would know if there was another."

Payton took the matchbook out of my hand. "There's another Brown Derby. Look." She pointed to a second address, then showed it to Margot.

"That's downtown."

"Do you think Leo will take us there?" I asked.

"Maybe," Margot said. "It could expand his delivery zone, which would mean more customers."

I signaled Leo on the walkie and within a minute he was at the corner of Hollywood and Vine.

Just as we got into the Burrito Taxi I saw Harry. "Don't look now," I said to Payton.

"Hurry!" Payton yelled at Leo. "Go! *Allez! Vámonos.*" She mocked his signature trio of phrases. Margot climbed in the plexiglass dome. She buckled herself, slid on goggles and her headphones. Payton crinkled herself into the backseat, forgetting about rock-paper-scissors.

Leo pressed the gas and the Burrito Taxi took off with a screech of the tires.

"Who was that man?" Leo asked.

"We'll tell you on the way," I said.

"On the way where?"

I showed him the matchbook. "The Brown Derby in LA."

He asked, "Where did you get that?"

"From ABJ's house."

Margot's voice came through a little speaker in the taxi's ceiling. "They think it might be a clue to finding ABJ's lost money."

Payton exclaimed, "Has stepping on your feet taught you nothing?"

"Oops," Margot said.

"Lost? LOST? Did you say 'lost'?" Leo asked.

To Leo I said, "Don't ever tell her a secret."

"Point taken. But, Ginger, what's going on?" Leo asked, "Is the money *lost* . . . as in disappeared, vanished, kissed good-bye?"

"It's not so much *lost* as she just doesn't know where it is," I said.

"That sounds a lot like the definition of lost," Leo said.

"That's one way to look at it," Payton said. "But, scientifically speaking, if you know something exists, like let's say radon or carbon monoxide, but you can't see it, it's not lost."

"Nope," I said. "It's not."

"And," Payton continued, "If you have tools to find those things, like a radon detector, then you'll know where it is."

"Totally," I agreed.

"So, the radon isn't lost, it just temporarily can't be located, but it will be," Payton said. "That's the kind of situation we're in with ABJ's life's savings."

"Eeeeexactly," I summed up. "Well said."

"Okay. Let's say I go with your little tale of weird science. That would mean you have a money detector. And if you do, I am leaving this Burrito Taxi right here, right now, and I'll sell money detectors."

Margot chimed in, "I haven't seen a money detector. I definitely wouldn't have been able to keep that a secret."

"It's the old-fashioned kind." I paused to snatch a look at the legendary Roxy Theatre—a famous concert place in West Hollywood—as we passed. "A paper with clues." I told him about ABJ thinking the bank was stealing and leaving herself an encrypted message.

"The bank wasn't stealing; they were deducting her mortgage payment. I helped her set that up." He thought for a minute. "She left herself a clue?"

I took the ripped paper out of my pocket and showed it to him. He waited until we had a red light and looked at it.

"So, we think it's hidden by a famous *D*," Payton said. "That's what we've been looking for at the wax museum, the Walk of Fame, and the Dolby Theatre."

"Then, last night, she slipped this matchbook into my hand when no one was looking. So I think she wants us to look at the Brown Derby," I said. "And it's also a *D*."

"That's what it looks like to me too," Leo said. "But there's nothing at the Brown Derby." He put the note down when the light turned green.

"We won't know for sure until we look," I said. "This is how detectives work. I've seen lots of black and white

Dick Tracy movies with Mom. Dick chases down every lead."

"I believe you. But if Dick Tracy had the Internet, he'd have checked the places he was going to in order to find out if they were still in business," Leo said. "The Brown Derby closed a long time ago—"

I let out a big exhale of frustration, while Payton sort of groaned.

"Now tell me who that guy was and why his pants were pulled up so high?"

"His name is Harry. He works at the Dolby. He's chasing us because we might have told one of his tours that the theater is haunted and he canceled the tour and called in paranormal experts who figured out there are no ghosts and now he's mad at us," I said.

"That's just a guess," Payton confirmed. "And the pants are a mystery that defies even the sharpest scientific minds."

"You don't have to have a science head to see that the wedgie is a major problem," I said. "It could actually cause a serious injury."

18

"How did it go today?" ABJ sat on her living room sofa, her legs crossed like she was posing for a photograph. "Are you making any progress?" She held a mirror with a delicate silver handle and made ridiculous faces at her reflection.

"We're progressing our way through Hollywood," I said.

"That's for sure," Payton said.

ABJ stared at herself. She opened her mouth as big as it could possibly go, and then tried to open it wider.

"The Dolby is beautiful," I added, still watching her unusual activity.

"Too bad it's haunted." Payton laughed halfheartedly because she, too, was focused on ABJ's reflection.

"I've never heard that." ABJ sucked her cheeks in like a fish and held them there.

"Oh, there are rumors," I said.

"More than rumors," Payton said. "They brought in an official paranormal investigator."

"To study the spirits," I said.

"You know, there could be more than one."

"Very true—" I started.

ABJ relaxed her cheeks and shifted her gaze from the mirror to us. "I understood at 'haunted.'" She sucked in her cheeks again.

"What are you doing?" I finally asked.

She attempted to talk with her face squished in, but all that came out were sucking and squirting sounds. She gave up and relaxed her face. "I'm exercising. There are forty-three muscles in the face, and as an actress, I like to keep them all strong." She looked at her reflection again. "My agent could call anytime."

"Do you talk to your agent often?"

"The agent-client relationship doesn't thrive on frequent communication. She's probably looking for the perfect opportunity. So I need to be ready." She added, "And, of course, negotiating a star on the Walk of Fame isn't easy."

"Being prepared is always good." I felt sad, because I thought ABJ's face was the only thing ready for an audition.

"Wow," Payton said. "That would be amazing. Your agent is doing that for you?"

"It is the highest honor. I'm certain she is working her magic," ABJ said.

I thought maybe her agent wasn't working on anything for ABJ. I considered mentioning that she should contact her agent, but I decided to put that idea in *mentalus storageum.*

"Anyway, tomorrow we're going to check out Rodeo Drive and the Hollywood sign. They're both famous and both have a *D* in their name. How do those two sound to you?" Payton asked.

"Well, I've spent a lot of time on Rodeo Drive. Shopping, you know."

"Do you have a favorite store?" Payton asked.

"Where to start . . . Burberry, Cartier, Chanel, Gucci, Tory Burch, Louis Vuitton, Prada, and of course Tiffany & Co."

"Like the movie?" I asked. *"Breakfast at Tiffany's?"*

"Just like that, except that was in New York City."

"That's a lot of ground to cover," Payton said.

"To pick any one favorite store just feels wrong." ABJ extended her forehead, and pulled it down to force her brow over tops of her eyes. Then she suddenly stopped. "Oh, I know what might help!"

"What?" Payton and I asked together.

"My closet! We can see where I buy most of my clothes. *That* would be my favorite store."

"Great plan," I said.

"You can do your facial workout in your room, while we gather data," Payton said.

"We'll make a bar graph."

"Or a line graph—" I said.

"Or a pie chart—" Payton said.

"To show which brand ABJ chose most, indicating which store on Rodeo Drive she went to most often."

"Then we'll know where to focus tomorrow," Payton suggested.

"Eeeeexactly," I agreed.

ABJ led us across the marble foyer, her silky robe flowing behind her like a bride's train, into the master bedroom suite. She flung aside the heavy tapestries covering a big picture window and let in a flood of warm sun. Then, with two hands, she dramatically opened her closet, although *closet* was not the right word. It was bigger than my pink bedroom.

Payton's mouth dropped open. "Two words: fashion awesomeness." She ran to the perimeter, extended her hand, and walked around letting her fingers touch every shirt, skirt, dress, pants, and gown, many of which were covered in plastic wrap, like it had come right from the dry cleaners, while others were in sturdy zippered bags.

I sat at a table in the middle of the closet. It was covered with little gold boxes filled with make up—lipstick, eye shadow, blushes, powders, pencils, and brushes of every shape and size. On a glass tray sat perfumes—bottles from the store, and crystal bottles with squeeze-y things to spritz. There was a neat row of hairspray, mousse, gel, and hair glitter. On each side of the table—front, left, and right—stood lighted mirrors illuminating every imperfection of my face and hair from every possible angle. I like my regular mirror from home better.

ABJ came in the closet, and closed the doors behind her. On the backs of the doors were more mirrors.

Payton gasped. "Oh no. Oh no. This isn't happening."

"What? Don't even tell me it's another ghost," I joked.

"The ghost was pretend. Remember? But *this* is real." She stared at a square column about six feet tall. It spun with just the slightest touch. On all four sides were cubbies.

Tidily tucked away in each were shoes! "Tell me I'm awake, not daydreaming, not imagining this."

"If you're dreaming, then I am too."

She picked up a sequined stiletto heel with ribbon straps and held it to her nose. "It doesn't smell pretend." She looked inside the shoe and teared up. "It's Choo."

"Bless you."

"No, these are *Jimmy* Choo." She showed me the label on the shoes.

I'd heard of Jimmy Choo, but I'd never actually seen a pair in person. From Payton's reaction, I'm guessing she hadn't either. After eying the sparkling heel for another second, Payton gasped again. "Oh no!"

"What now?" I asked.

"They're a size EIGHT!" Payton and I were both a size eight.

ABJ sat on a chaise lounge and curled her legs under herself. "Try them on," she said.

"Really?" Payton asked.

"Truly?" I asked.

"Have fun."

And try them on we did.

Everything.

"Which dress would your wear to the ceremony for your new star?" I asked her.

"Oh, none of these. I would get something designed special." She added, "Probably I would find some new up-and-coming designer and give him or her a boost in their career."

"So, you've thought about it?" Payton asked.

"Of course. I'm an actress, after all." She watched us trying on all her fancy clothes and jewels. "I remember your mother doing the same thing when she was your age, only her feet were already a size nine, so all the shoes hurt her."

We modeled the outfits, took pictures, and most importantly, kept a list of the brand names. ABJ put a tick mark after the ones that had multiple articles of clothing. She had a system of making four vertical tick marks and then a fifth one diagonally across, making little batches of fives. My brain tingled: the batches looked just like the little hay bales on the ripped paper clue. I filed that deet in my *mentalus storageum*, I definitely needed to think about it later, but right now I was playing dress-up—big girl style.

Not five minutes later we were dressed to the nines. I was ready for a black-tie ball, while Payton donned cruise wear. Complete with a visor and tennis racquet.

"You look like a million bucks," Payton said, flipping the label of the dress I was wearing. "Literally."

"Who ever thought that collecting raw data could be so glam?" I asked.

"And the fun is just beginning," Payton said. "We still get to do the analysis."

"Maybe not—" I held our hay bales of raw data. "I don't think we're gonna need to chart to show us which store."

The winner was clear: Dior.

"D," Payton said. "I think I just gave myself chills."

I asked ABJ, "What do you think about Dior?"

She was staring in her mirror again. "Think? I think it's good. Easter is good, too."

"Easter? What?" Payton asked.

I looked at her closely. "I think she's tired."

"I guess hours of dress-up, I mean research, will do that," Payton said.

"You want to lie down?"

"As beautiful as an Easter lily," ABJ mumbled. "I went to the Derby on Easter."

She must have some wonderful memories of the Brown Derby. I didn't have the heart to tell her that it was closed.

19

⌒‿⌒

We got into our pajamas. All the while we could hear Grant say, "Eeew! Gross!" Then take a break. Then, "Eeew! Ugh! Yuck!"

"What do you think he's doing?" Payton asked.

I barged in without knocking, and Payton followed. He had an iPad on his lap, eyes covered, but watching something through the cracks of his fingers. He clicked his fingers back together and said, "Oh man. Gross."

"What on earth are you watching?" Payton asked.

"It's not from Earth. It's an alien autopsy. Dr. Evans is removing each body part."

"Really?" I asked, and took the iPad from him.

"Hey!"

"Oh puh-lease. You were hardly watching it," Payton said. "Besides, this could be important research for the Science Olympics, which we have to get cranking on, Ging."

"I know. I know."

Payton and I watched Dr. Evans saw the alien skull and remove the brain.

My medulla oblongata tingled. "I just got an idea of how our project can be *ooh la la*."

"A model of an alien brain?" Payton asked.

"Not exactly, but that's good too." I filed that idea.

"Give it back." Grant grabbed the iPad.

"I'll get the supplies," Payton said, "and you can fill me in."

"Now?" I asked. "It's late. What about the five a.m. schedule?"

"We have"—Payton looked at the app—"seventy-nine hours. And we'll probably spend about twenty-four of those sleeping and twenty-one of them searching for a hidden treasure, that might be hidden, might not. We don't really know. All we have to go on is a half chewed-up paper clue, that might be a clue, but might not. We're not sure."

"I'm sure," I said.

"But we really don't know. ABJ doesn't even know for sure," Payton said.

"Whoa," Grant said. "Are you guys bickering?"

I yelled at Payton, "If you don't want to look for the money, you don't have to!"

Grant said, "You are so bickering."

"If we were Olympic figure skaters who were treasure hunting, or whatever, during the day, do you think we would practice at night?" Payton yelled back.

Grant turned on his iPad's camera. "I'm gonna record this."

"No, you're not." I snatched it out of his hand. "And we are not bickering." I asked Payton, "Are we?"

"No." She sighed. "I'm just tired and I'm worried about the Olympics." Then she added, "You know how the DeMarcos get under my skin."

"I'm tired too," I assured her. "You think I want to lose to the DeMarcos?"

Grant said, "DeFart-Os." Then he started watching the alien autopsy again.

"No. I know you don't want to lose."

"But this thing with ABJ is really important too. I mean, she could lose *her house*!"

"I get it. I get it," Payton said. "But it's frustrating to be grasping at straws."

"Now we have Dior, maybe that won't be a straw."

"Maybe," she agreed.

"And if we drink espresso and eat chocolate, we'll get energy to work on the project tonight," I assured her.

"Good plan."

20

As expected, a Burrito Taxi with a sidecar fringed with plastic shredded lettuce didn't blend in at the intersection of Rodeo Drive and Wilshire Boulevard. Leo dropped me, Payton, and Margot off in front of a grand hotel displaying multiple flags on its front facade: the Beverly Wilshire Hotel. My mom knew it well from the famous movie *Pretty Woman*. It's what she calls "a modern classic."

The clean sidewalk bustled with shoppers in high heels and big purses.

"Pickpockets make a fortune on streets like this," Margot said. "Tuck your money deep down and don't let anyone bump into you."

She is usually a pessimist, but in this case she had a point, so I pushed my thirteen dollars to the bottom of my front pocket.

Margot scanned the street again. "Tsk," she said.

"What is it?" I asked.

"Just that there aren't enough fire hydrants. I mean, there are the required amounts, but on crowded streets like this, there really should be extra, in case there are two fires at the same time, you know?" Margot asked.

I thought that the Los Angeles Fire Department probably had all their bases covered, but I had no knowledge of fire preparedness, so I just said, "Uh-huh."

Leo handed out business cards to the uniformed bellhops guarding the front entrance as if it was Buckingham Palace. They politely declined the offer. "Not my target market," Leo said to us.

"Indeed, I should think not," Payton said in a hoity-toity British accent that captured the tone of the fancy-pants people and cars around us.

"Yes, dahling, let's talk like that on Rodeo Drive," I said.

"Brilliant plan," Payton said.

Then Margot tried, "And we can send the butler to the carriage house for some porridge." It was a good first try.

Dior wouldn't be hard to find since the luxury shopping area was only about three blocks long. The street was lined in palm trees, and people carried large paper shopping bags.

Dior had an elegant storefront with dangerously skinny mannequins in the windows. Their hair was long and poker straight, their sunglasses huge and round. What caught my eye more than the life-size Barbies were the white lights woven throughout the display. It gave me an idea for our project that I tucked among the other stuff cluttering my *mentalus storageum*.

Payton opened the door and held it for us. "After you, dahlings."

"Why, thank you. You are too kind," I said.

"Why yes . . . you are . . . you are . . . sweet as an English meadow with . . . with . . . porridge." Margot broke character. "I'm running out of ideas."

"It happens," I said. "Keep trying. It gets easier."

Once in the store, I admired the sparkling metal of the racks and the shine on the white floor. "Now, start looking. And act natural."

Within a minute of starting our serious hunting mode, the only customer left the store, leaving it practically silent.

A saleswoman in a tight black dress and an equally tight updo asked, "May I help you?"

"Oh. You see it's Mum's birthday." Payton looked at her name tag. "Ms. Taggart, is it? Would it be improper if I were to refer to you as Grace?"

"That would be fine."

"Lovely. Well, I thought a wee bit of perfume or a grand scarf would be brilliant. Do you think she would fancy that?" Payton asked.

Grace led Payton to the perfume counter while Margot and I continued to sleuth. I hunted for a box, a closet, a space of any kind that might be suitable for safekeeping a treasure, but the store was sparse, with only a few round racks and wall hangers.

I patted the wall space behind each of the hangers to feel for a door, but there was only wall. Then, I thought, maybe it only *looks like* a wall. I've watched enough episodes of classic *Batman* to know that all it takes is one lever to open a secret door with poles that you slide down to get to a cave. I started touching anything I could get my hands on.

Grace sprayed a ribbon with fragrance and held it out for Payton to sniff.

While Payton considered her options, Grace bent down to where Margot was crawling under some cocktail dresses. "Looking for something?"

I held my breath. *Is Margot going to be able to think fast?*

"Indeed I am." Margot started out strong. "If I may be quite frank with you, Miss Taggart. There's a problem."

There is?

"There is?"

"Yes, ma'am, madam, m'dam." Margot stumbled a little. "The problem is that I don't see what I am looking for." And she recovered.

"I am sure I can find anything we have in this store."

Even a hidden treasure?

"Precautions," Margot said. "Pre-cau-tions. Do you know what I mean?"

Huh?

"Pre . . . No. I don't," Grace said.

Where is Margot going with this?

Margot slid her headphones on and bent the microphone in front of her mouth. "Hello? Cheerio. Are you there?"

She pretended to listen to someone in her headset.

"I am at the location." She listened again. "I will, and

I will undoubtedly resume this conversation with you after tea and biscuits."

Tea and biscuits? Not bad, Margot.

To Grace she explained, "I . . . we . . . are undercover inspectors with the Office of Safety Inspections for Retail Establishments National."

"SIREN," Payton confirmed, coming up behind us.

I added, "You have most certainly heard SIREN's work in the area of *precautions.*"

"No." Grace put her hands on her hips. "What are you girls, thirteen? And you're British. I don't believe you're working with any US office of any kind. Are you trying to steal something? I can call the police right now."

Oh, that would be just great! The LAPD probably already has a complaint from the Dolby Theatre about girls pretending to be paranormal investigators.

Margot laughed with a snort. "Steal?" She laughed again. "You see, my fair maiden . . . there is . . . umm . . . porridge . . . and the carriage house . . ."

Porridge signaled that things were heading south.

"Precisely correct," I helped her. "The US office is in a carriage house in Washington, DC, which is where teens are trained to be undercover operatives over school breaks. They quite fancy teens because they go undetected."

Margot added, "Easier to be undercover if you're undetected. Don't you fancy?"

"Seems foreign teens are even more undetectable," Payton said. "Now, let us tend to the matter at hand, which is the *precautions*." To Margot she asked, "Are you going to explain the problem, Lady Buckingham?"

Margot tossed her hands up. "There aren't any! There are no safety precautions anywhere that I can see. And without such measures in place to protect your customers from fires, hurricanes, tsunamis, tarantulas, monsoons, sandstorms, floods—"

"We're in California," Grace complained. "Floods are unlikely."

"My good lady," Payton explained. "The precaution epidemic is nationwide."

"Fine." Grace rolled her eyes. "So what happens without the precautions?"

"You get a ticket, a fine, and a strongly worded letter," Margot said.

"Okay," Grace said. "Just give it to me, and get going."

We can't leave without more searching.

"And," I added. "As the lady of the store, your photo will be posted on SIREN's website, and Dior is required to dismiss you."

"What? I lose my job?"

"It isn't personal, milady madam," Margot said. "It is in the statute."

"I get a forty percent discount!"

"That is a fancy percentage. Can't we help her?" Payton asked Margot.

"I think perhaps . . ." Margot looked around the store. "We may find some precautions, if we simply look carefully enough."

"Oh yes!" I agreed. "We had grand luck at Saks Fifth Avenue when they had their Jimmy Choo precaution problem."

"So let's help her and have a careful look, shall we?" Margot said, "Don't fret, my good lady, my lass, we are trained for this. With a little luck, we'll find enough precautions for you to keep your station."

"Fine. Look."

I felt bad lying to Grace like that, but it really was fun.

I asked, "Are there storage spaces or hidden chambers? Passageways?"

"There's a small closet in the back room where we keep holiday decorations."

"Blimey!" Payton exclaimed. "There could be one there. Let's look."

We followed her into a room where it looked like employees could eat lunch. "There." She pointed to a closet door covered with all types of employment-related signs, IF YOU GET HURT AT WORK . . . , TEN WAYS TO SPOT SHOP-LIFTING. And big words said, THINK OF YOURSELF AS A CUSTOMER.

"Do you have a key to that padlock?"

"Only the manager does. And she won't be in today."

"Then I suppose our work here is done," Margot said. She moved the mic to her mouth.

Payton said, "What a pity to lose that forty percent. Tsk. Tsk."

"No!" Grace cried. "Let's get that lock open."

"Brilliant idea," Payton said.

The sales clerk dumped out a box of tools that she found under a sink. A pair of bolt cutters was among the pile.

"This will work lovely," British Payton said, then she wrapped the cutter around the lock and *snap!* It came loose.

I saw a tub at the bottom of the pile labeled DERBY DAY. I figured they were decorations related to the Kentucky Derby horse race . . . but *derby* . . . like Brown Derby . . . and a *D* . . . actually two *D*s.

Hmmm. Maybe we were onto something.

I moved the boxes labeled CHRISTMAS, VALENTINE'S DAY, and FOURTH OF JULY onto the floor until I got to the dusty Derby Day box.

I cracked open the lid and peeked inside.

First I saw feathers.

Then I saw hats—wide-brimmed hats dressed up with feathers and flowers. The kind worn to the Kentucky Derby. These were probably for mannequins.

"Not here," I said to Payton.

Grace slumped. "No precautions at all?"

"This happens sometimes. Terribly sorry, my good lady." Payton moved back toward the front of the store. I followed her.

Grace sniffled. "Bye-bye, forty percent."

"Wait." Margot looked serious. To Grace she said, "Oh rubbish! I'm not going to call this in. You are a good lady. I cannot bare to see you removed from your station." To us she said, "I fancy making an exception."

We left the store with only a paisley scarf for Mum's birthday.

"You just shocked the heck out of me," I said to Margot.

"I shocked ME," she said. "That was so, so, so much fun. Can we do it again?"

"But of course, dahling." I dramatically swept the scarf around my neck and lifted my knee, offering it in a knee high-five to both of them.

21

Leo asked, "Where to next?"

I pointed up to the hills to the Hollywood sign snuggled behind a mix of clouds and smog. "That's the last *D* on our list."

"Oh, well that's gonna be difficult," Leo said.

"Why?" I asked.

"I'll explain in the car," Leo said. "If we park somewhere else, I can sell a few burritos while we talk. Ain't nobody on this street buys food from the back of a taxi."

I opened the passenger door of the Burrito Taxi and put my arm behind my back.

"One-two-three-shoot!"

Payton put out paper.

I put out rock.

"Ugh." I was in the back. This time I laid on my back and pulled my knees up to my chest. It wasn't too bad, except I couldn't see out the window.

Payton looked at her phone as Leo drove up Wilshire Boulevard. "Wait. Where are you going? My GPS says the sign is the other way."

"I told you it would be difficult. It's closed to the public, surrounded by a razor-wire fence, and monitored by motion detector cameras that feed into police headquarters."

"Well that's discouraging," I said.

"Sounds impossible," Payton added.

The speaker in the ceiling said, "Difficult, not impossible."

It was kind of creepy the way she could hear us without being in the taxi.

"So where are we going?" Payton asked.

"To the police station," Leo said.

"Why?" Payton asked.

"They like burritos."

I stared at the roof of the taxi and took stock of my situation:

- My Science Olympics project was worked out in my head, but we didn't have time to work on it and time was ticking. I thought it was very likely that we were going to lose the bet with the DeMarcos, which would lead to Payton *totally* freaking out.

- We had only one place left to hunt for a treasure that was maybe buried somewhere in Hollywood, possibly near a famous *D*. A treasure that, as Payton pointed out, might not be hidden at all; it might've been spent or stolen. And we only had a ripped clue, which we were not even sure was a clue at all, to work with.

- Chances were that after spring break, Payton and I were going to lose to the DeMarcos. I would run home from school, humiliated, and bury my head in my pillow, which would now reside in an outer-space-themed room that I shared with the only nine-year-old to be on the FBI's list of suspected aliens. And ABJ would be unpacking her Hollywood memorabilia in her new pink room.

- I was balled-up, staring at the ceiling of a banana pretending to be a burrito.

A feeling of impending doom warmed me—*or is that the temperature in the back of this vehicle?*

"We're almost there," Leo said. "I'll just heat up our supply and we'll be ready to go." He pushed a button and hot air filled the taxi with the smell of ground beef with taco seasoning.

"Can I get a little air conditioning back here?"

"Sure," Leo opened the window and a burst of hot air flowed through my hair.

He stuck his arm out and waved to people as we passed. "Hey, bud!" "Hey, dude!" "Hiya!" "Text me!" "See you later!" "Howdy!"

He pulled over at the police station among a row of food trucks. Payton helped me roll out, and we met Margot and Payton at the popped trunk. Instantly a cloud of Mexican deliciousness lured a swarm of uniformed people in our direction.

"My friends in blue," Leo said. "As always, a lunch special for you who protect and serve."

"What's the special today?" asked an officer whose breast was heavily adorned with patches and symbols.

"Half price." Leo's announcement was met with a crowd of claps. "My young friends here"—Leo indicated us—"will get you whatever you want." He collected money while we handed out foil-wrapped lunches to everyone.

"These ladies are visiting all the way from Delaware. They want to be doctors, and they're working on an amazing science project at their great-aunt's house up in the hills."

The cops unwrapped their burritos and listened to Leo, who seemed to have a way of capturing people's attention. "They've been a huge help to her—she's having some health issues."

"It's nice to hear that today's youth still helps their aging family members," said one officer.

"Yeah," Leo said. "They're actually helping her find something very important that she's lost. They've spent their whole spring break searching high and low—"

Leo was interrupted by a symphony of police radios. "All units! Please respond to a ten ninety-nine at Hollywood and Vine."

Leo received a stream of backslaps and thank-yous. Only one officer remained.

"Why don't you need to respond to the call?" I asked him.

"I'm a bicycle cop. We don't respond to ten ninety-nines." He took the last bite of his burrito. "Good batch today, Leo."

"Thanks, Mitch," Leo said. "Actually, you were the guy I came here to see, but I thought I'd sell a few burritos too."

"Really? Me? How come?"

"You still taking the tour shuttles up to the sign?"

"Every Saturday and Sunday. Student loans, you know."

"Sure. I get it." Leo added, "I would be very appreciative to anyone who could help these girls."

"Tell me whatcha need. I might be persuaded." He shoved the burrito in his mouth and paused for only a second to appreciate the flavor. "Really good batch," Mitch said again.

22

I don't know how we did it, but Payton and I were *both* in the backseat. I tried to sit in the plexiglass sidecar with Margot, but the extra weight made it sag to the pavement.

My legs hung over the front seat, one on each side of Leo's head. Payton's did the same to Mitch the bicycle cop. It was the only way we could fit.

"We'll pick up a shuttle bus. That will be less conspicuous than this taxi," Mitch said.

"Good plan," Payton said, but getting words out when your body was so compacted wasn't easy.

"Air," I managed to push out.

Leo and Mitch opened their windows.

"You know," Mitch said. "I'd love to get into this business with you."

"Seriously?" Leo asked. "I've been thinking of expanding. The problem has been acquiring a second vehicle. Finding automobiles shaped like Mexican food is harder than you'd expect."

"Well, you might be in luck. We impounded a Wiener Mobile about ten years back. It was never picked up and is about to go to auction."

"You canNOT be serious."

"I would never joke about a Wiener Mobile."

"If you get these girls to that *D*, and get that mobile at the auction, you've got a deal," Leo said.

Margot's voice chimed in overhead, "Pending a full safety inspection of the wiener."

"Isn't that obvious?" Mitch said up into the speaker. "I can get you to the *D*. Consider this a done deal."

We wound up roads that made the taxi feel more like a roller coaster than a food car. The serpentine turns made my stomach flip-flop in an unpleasant way, risking serious burrito puke in the back of this mobile. I didn't tell Payton, because that puke was going to affect her way more than it would me.

"Are we there yet?" I asked.

"I might barf," Payton said. Me and my bestie are so much alike.

"Almost, little grasshoppers." Leo wasn't lying because the taxi stopped at a parking lot of shuttle buses labeled HOLLYWOOD SIGN TOURS.

"Lemme get the keys," Mitch said.

"Where are we going?" I asked.

"All the way to the *D*, I hope." Leo rubbed his palms together. "Did you hear about the wiener? This is a great day."

"If we find what we want at the *D*, it will be an *amazing* day," I agreed.

Margot said, "Utterly smashing, dahling. Perhaps there will even be porridge there."

Payton said, "I don't think we're doing that anymore."

"Right." Margot shrugged. "I was just practicing."

A second later we were riding in style in an air-conditioned shuttle bus with cushy seats. I had my own seat.

Mitch filled us in on his tour spiel. "This mountain that the Hollywood sign sits on is called Mount Lee. The letters are forty-five feet tall each, the whole sign is three-hundred-fifty feet long, and it sits in the middle of Griffith Park, which was an ostrich farm in the 1800s. The park and the Griffith Observatory have been featured in Hollywood films, but none more prominently then James Dean's 1955 *Rebel Without a Cause*. The sign was originally built in 1923 as an advertisement for a real estate development and cost twenty-one thousand dollars. It was only intended to last for a year and a half, but it became an internationally recognized symbol during the Golden Age of Hollywood and was left there."

Very interesting stuff. Suddenly I was bummed about not taking any actual tours in Hollywood.

Mitch continued, "Originally the sign was built with no access. Since there were no streets, mules brought the building supplies up the hill, but in 1940 Howard Hughes bought the one hundred and thirty-eight acres around the sign to build a fantastic mansion for his fiancée, Ginger Rogers."

"I was named after her!" I yelled out.

"Then Hollywood is in your blood," Mitch said. "Howard Hughes built the access roads for the project, but he and Ginger broke up and the mansion was never built. But people say *something* was built, only no one knows what because Howard was real secretive—kind of a strange guy, a real 'end-of-the-world nut.' Anyway, soon the sign became a target of vandals and pranksters."

Margot said, "Lots of them got hurt."

Mitch nodded. "So access was limited and eventually made illegal."

"If it's illegal, how are we going to get to the *D* in the sign?" I asked.

"You might want to pull this bus over right now. Uncle Leo and I aren't doing anything that even smells like it might be illegal," Margot said. "What kind of cop are you?"

"Whoa, calm down there, Susie Safetypants. No one is doing anything illegal. I have no intention of breaking the oath I took as a bicycle cop," Mitch said. "I gotta ask you though, have you got something against *L*s? There are two of them, you know? Right next to each other."

Margot started, "The hidden—"

Payton swung her foot into Margot's shin, maybe a little harder than she intended, because Margot winced. "Nothing against them," Payton said. "But the letter *D* is special to us."

"Then I'm the man who can get you there. You see, when our old friend Howard Hughes didn't build the mansion of love for Ginger, the city bought the land and installed a radio tower to control all of the police communications."

"How does that get us closer to the sign?" I said.

"No one can get to the letters except radio tower maintenance or police," Mitch said. He flashed his police badge. "I'm your man."

Now I understood why Leo went to the police station. "That's what I'm talking about," I said.

Payton said, "We won't even have to pretend anything is possessed or haunted."

"Or lacking precautions," Margot added.

"What?" Leo asked. "What was pretend haunted?"

"Long story," I said.

"You wouldn't have to fake it here," Mitch said. "There has long been talk of this area being haunted by the ghost of Peg Entwistle."

"Who's that?" Payton asked.

"An actress. She died back in 1932. By the *H*."

A chill went up my back. That's the way it always worked in the movies—pretending all this time, and now something was *actually* haunted. I shook it off as we started for the sign.

23

With Mitch's keys, swipe cards, and secret passwords, we got into the restricted area, up to the radio tower, through the razor-wire fence, and we hiked down to the letters.

The sound of a police radio squeaked. "Unit B-Nineteen, please check in."

"That's me," Mitch said. "B is for bicycle." Into the police radio that was attached to his shoulder he said, "B-Nineteen."

"Are you in the restricted area?"

"That's affirmative," Mitch said.

"Did she say this is restricted? Then we can't be here." Margot tugged Leo's arm. "Come on, we can't stay."

The radio asked, "Do you have clearance?"

"That's affirmative." Then to Margot he said, "We have clearance."

"Oh. I love *affirmative*," Margot said.

"So much better than *negative*," Payton said.

"Or *no*," I said.

"Or *not now*."

"Or *never*."

Suddenly Mitch stopped walking. "Is this like a routine you're practicing?"

"It's for real, dude," Leo said. "They're trying to break the habit, but haven't been having much luck."

"I don't know why it bothers people so much," I said.

"I know. Right?" Payton asked.

"I mean, can't we open our minds, people?"

"A little tolerance."

"It makes us special," Payton said.

"No two snowflakes are the same, and that makes them special," I said.

"And you don't see anyone getting their neurotransmitters in a twist over that," Payton said.

"Somehow snowflakes can be unique, but as soon as two besties finish each other's thoughts, there's a protest," I said.

Margot jumped in, "Did someone in government sign a referendum stating that friends who quick-talk phrases is a public health crisis?"

Huh?

"That didn't make sense, did it?" she asked.

"I just like that you try," Payton said.

I said, "Me too. If at first you don't succeed—"

"Enough!" Mitch said at the front of the first O in *WOOD*. "If you three can't zip it, I'm turning my shuttle around and taking you out of here. No Wiener Mobile could be worth this."

"Jeez," I whispered to Payton.

"Testy," Payton whispered back.

"Grumpster," Margot said. (*She did it!*)

Leo zippered his mouth and pointed at us.

We okay-signed back to him.

"Here we are." We'd walked three hundred and fifty feet, and now Mitch stopped by the *D*. "Do your thing."

I looked up at the massive letter and had a vague feeling I was on an episode of *Sesame Street* that was sponsored by the letter *D*.

I said, "Let's get to work." We felt all over the *D* itself. Well, the bottom five feet of it. It towered over us, not unlike a skyscraper. If I jumped as far as I could, I wouldn't have reached the hole in the D. We went around back and felt the rods and poles and posts supporting the massive letter.

I didn't see or feel any levers or compartments.

"Anything?" I asked Payton.

She shook her head.

I looked at Leo to see if he'd found anything. "Nada. Zip. Doughnut," he said.

I propped my hands on my hips. "What about the pirate way?"

"Buried?" Payton asked.

"If you have another idea, my auditory system is ready and waiting."

She twisted her earring. "I don't."

"Let's kick up some dirt." I grabbed a stick and poked it all around the ground under and surrounding the D.

Payton got on her hands and knees and moved big stones.

Nothing.

We stood together, and gazed down at the city. "Think," I said.

"My synapses are firing on full blast, but I'm not getting any other ideas."

"How would ABJ have gotten it up here?" I asked.

Mitch said, "You just have to know the right people."

"She doesn't know anyone," I said.

"That's not true," Leo said. "She just doesn't see anyone anymore. She knows lots of people in town and she still has lots of fans—she gets mail and everything."

"Maybe there are other sites that we haven't thought of," I said.

"Or, I hate to say it," Payton said, "but maybe the money really doesn't exist."

To Leo I asked, "Is that possible?"

"I guess anything is possible. She could have donated it or walked onto Hollywood Boulevard one day and tossed it in the air."

"People would've gotten trampled, and we would've heard about it on the news," Margot said. "I watch for things like that. Pretty much every day, someone somewhere has gotten trampled. Sometimes by people, but also by horses, elephants—one time it was a team of Labradoodles. Not a pretty sight."

Payton asked, "Do you ever think of sunshine and roses?"

"Sure. Sunshine gives you sunburn, which can lead to

melanoma. And roses have thorns that prick you, leaving open wounds that often get infected."

Leo, who led our hike back to the shuttle, said, "Since you were a little girl, you've always looked at the darkest side of things."

"I don't think of it as 'dark.' I like to consider all the possibilities so that I can be prepared. I wear sunscreen—one hundred SPF—and never touch roses. See how that works?"

When she explained it, it sort of made sense.

Mitch took us back to the taxi. Payton and I rock-paper-scissored while the men discussed Wiener Mobile deets.

24

Payton and I sat outside on the patio with Payton's laptop open to our original notes about searching in Hollywood.

Leo had dropped Margot off at home, and returned to ABJ's where he had housework to do.

"I think my ganglions are tangled from thinking about this so much," I said.

Payton said, "Look, I want to help ABJ keep her house and you keep your new bedroom, but we need to get our ganglions tangled around the Science Olympics."

"I know," I said. *I KNOW! I KNOW! How could I NOT know, when you've brought it up EVERY SINGLE DAY?!*

Payton asked, "How much time do we have now?"

I looked at my phone. "It's T minus fifty-five hours."

"Crap. Ginger, that might not be enough time."

I really didn't want to set the ABJ thing aside, but maybe it was good to give my temporal lobes a break from Ds, hay bales, and hash marks, and unpack the Science Olympics ideas that were crowding my *mentalus storageum*. I explained them to Payton.

"I like it," she said, then yelled into the kitchen to ask Leo, "Where does ABJ keep her Christmas decorations?"

"In the basement." He clarified, "Well, it's not exactly a basement. More of a basement-slash-fallout shelter. You see, this house was built in 1945, right after World War II, which was a time when people seriously prepared for a nuclear attack by building bomb shelters. Some people built them under their backyards, but basically anyplace they could dig deep enough and pour cement would work."

He opened a closet door in the kitchen and took a few steps down before pulling a string, which lit an overhead bulb, revealing a second door—the metal kind that looked like it led to a vault in a bank rather than to a basement. Leo twisted a latch, and with a pop and a sigh, the door swung open. We stepped down a few more times into the cement tomb.

Leo said, "She still keeps some food and water down

here in case of a storm or something, but it's not stocked like most people did when they were preparing for a nuclear blast."

There was a case of water bottles, and about ten gallon jugs. A metal shelf held canned foods, a radio, blankets, a few flashlights, batteries, basic tools, and some hygiene items.

There were three large metal benches that seemed like they could double as beds, if needed, but instead were used to hold cardboard boxes marked with a Sharpie. Most were movie titles that I recognized as those ABJ had been in.

There was also a tower of shoeboxes marked with dates: 1960–1963; 1967–1970; 1971–1974; and so on. I noticed that 1964–1966 was missing in the sequence. I took the lid off the one on top marked 1960–1963. Inside was a pile of photographs.

"Wow," Payton said. "Look at ABJ. She is beautiful now, but look at her here."

"She's so young," I said.

"Who are these men that she's with?"

"This is John Wayne," I said. "This one is Jimmy Stewart. And this one is Harry Cooper."

She gave me a look that said she was surprised that I knew this.

"Maybe I spend a little too much time with my mom," I said.

"I think this proves it," Payton said.

Leo slid some boxes around. "Here is Christmas. What are you looking for?"

I smiled. "Something to give the Science Olympics project more *umph*."

25

꒜

That evening we covered the patio table with supplies. Payton worked on a poster, while I used wire and electrical tape to get us closer to *ooh la la.*

Mom, Dad, and Grant came home with two steaming hot pizzas. I never thought I'd want a change from burritos, but the smell wooed Payton and I away from our project and woke ABJ from her nap. We congregated in the formal living room, where Leo handed out paper plates.

"Grant said he always wanted to eat in here," ABJ explained. I thought it was cute that she and Grant had become pals.

Hey, maybe she can share the alien room with him and I can keep my new pink room!

"Yup. On the white sofas!" Grant confirmed.

"Are you sure this is a good idea?" Dad asked ABJ.

"You only live once!" Then she whispered something to Leo, who left the room.

He returned a second later with sheets.

"Stand up for a sec," he said to us, and he tossed the sheets over the white sofa. We sat back down and he did the same to the chairs.

"Now. Who wants pepperoni?" ABJ asked and handed out slices to everyone.

Mom said, "We had the most amazing day."

"What did you do?" Payton asked.

"A tour of Universal Studios. I got to see the house from the movie *Psycho*. It's not quite as creepy in the middle of a sunny day, but surreal to see it in person."

"What else?"

"Then we did an open-air bus tour all over Hollywood and I learned so much."

"It could be because she asked a bazillion questions," Grant said. "People got off the bus to get away from her. It was so annoying."

"Oh, come on now. They had places they wanted to go see, while I wanted to hear everything. People tour in different ways." Then she began sharing tidbits of everything she'd learned. "Did you know they say that John Wayne might have kept a cow on his deck of the Sunset Hotel?"

"I didn't know that," I said.

"You knew John Wayne, didn't you, ABJ?" Payton asked.

"I think I may have met him once. It was 1962, I think."

She can remember that date, but not where she's hidden her life's fortune.

Mom told us more. "Let's see: Four stars have been stolen from the Walk of Fame. Can you imagine? And Hollywood itself was originally the site of a fig orchard. Oh, and did you know that the original title for *Ghostbusters* was *Ghost Smashers*?"

"Seems like you learned a lot today," I said.

Mom bit into her pepperoni pizza. "Ohh." She held up the one-finger giving herself a chance to swallow. "How cool is this: the Hollywood sign was built to advertise a real estate development!"

I said, "Actually, *that* I knew."

"Hollywoodland," Mom said. "That was the name of it. I want to get a poster of that."

"You mean there were four more letters?" I asked.

"Duh," Grant said. "L-A-N-D."

The hangman dashes! That's what those little lines were on the clue! Thirteen of them. A hash mark for every letter of the sign.

My brain tingled in places I didn't know it could tingle.

"Speaking of Mitch, can we call him?" I asked Leo.

"Who was talking about Mitch?" Leo asked.

"Who's Mitch?" Mom asked.

Leo asked, "Why?"

I ticked off on my fingers and spelled, "L-A-N-D."

Payton gasped. "There's another *D*!"

26

On Thursday morning the countdown app said forty hours—just two days left. I'd wiggled all night, thinking about the second *D*. I couldn't wait to check it out.

While Payton and I waited for Leo to see Mitch, we *kapow*-ed our Science Olympics project.

"I can't wait to see the DeMarcos' face when the judges announce us as the winners," Payton said.

"When they lose the bet, we're going to see a lot more than their faces."

"I know. Right?"

Since Dad fixed the slamming front door, we smelled Leo and Margot before we heard them.

"Am I smelling what I think I'm smelling?" Payton asked.

"If you think it's bacon, then yes."

Margot said, "If you think it's lima beans, then no."

Payton took a foil packet. "Bacon on a breakfast burrito is a good thing."

"Bacon on pretty much everything is a good thing," I agreed.

"I know. Right?"

"And it's the main contributor to high blood pressure, which is a leading indicator of stroke and heart attack, but hey, don't let that stop you."

"I won't," I said.

"I made one hundred of them!" Leo said. "Once I let the smell of these babies float out of my trunk and onto the Hollywood streets, they'll sell themselves."

"Can we eat them on the road?" I said. "I want to get up that mountain again."

"I just need my sneakers and then I'm ready," Payton said.

"Me too," I said. "And let's leave a burrito next to ABJ's bed so she'll smell it first thing when she wakes up."

"She'll love that!" Payton said.

"I'll do it while you get your sneakers," Margot said.

We were just finishing up when Margot yelled from ABJ's bedroom, "She's gone!"

27

I asked, "She's not here?"

Leo said, "This isn't the first time this has happened. We need to ABJ-proof this house: alarms, locks, cowbell."

"Where do you think she went?" Payton asked.

"Maybe looking for the money?" Leo suggested.

"Or maybe she went to the Derby for Easter," I said.

"Or maybe the Dolby for an award show," Payton said.

"Or maybe—"

PSSSHT! PSSSHT!

The walkie in Leo's pocket was receiving a signal.

"This is the next best thing to a cowbell, I guess," he said. "It must be her."

I took it out of his hand. "ABJ, is that you? Where are you?" I asked.

"No. This is Patel Poplawski. I work at the Bounce Land in Studio City. We have a lady here who will not get off our Velcro wall. She wants you to come get her," he said. "I need to call the police. She is interrupting a party."

"Patel Poppy? Is that you? This is Leo. The one who owns the Burrito Taxi."

"Hey! Leo Leo Burrito! What you up to, my main man? I have not seen you in a long time."

Leo directed us toward the front door. "Well, you're going to see me in about eight minutes to pick up that lovely woman, who is a close personal friend." He rushed us into the taxi as he spoke. I thought that I wanted a turn sitting in the sidecar, but this wasn't the time to bring that up. I jumped into the back, without rock-paper-scissors.

Leo said into the walkie, "Can you hold off on calling the police, the fuzz, the boys in blue?" He hit the gas and the taxi took off with the velocity of a straw popping out of a juice box that's been squeezed.

"Leo, my friend, the children want to use the Velcro wall. I do not have a choice."

"Do those children like bacon?"

"Hold on. I shall ask them."

Leo wove through the traffic of commuters trying to get to the CBS Studio Center, and tourists wanting a glimpse of the house from the 1970s TV show *The Brady Bunch*.

"They say they *do* like bacon," Patel said.

"Well, then they are in for a very nice surprise." Leo added, "Hey, P. Poppy, why do you have a party there so early in the morning?"

"It is this kid's birthday. His mom had to have a party on his *actual* birthday. Wouldn't wait until Saturday. You know the type?"

"I do, P. Pop. I do."

"And the kid has violin after school," Patel Poplawski said. "Can you feel my pain, man?"

"I feel it, P. Pop." Leo asked, "How's your mom?"

"She is good. You know always with the bunions. But she started dancing lessons—the salsa kind. Can you believe that? She could use a friend to dance with, though. You know what I mean? She always wants to go with me. And me, both of my feet are on the left."

"Oh, I'm sure that's not true." Leo took a sharp corner onto a street. On both sides poked a straight row of very tall palm trees spaced far apart. "You probably dance like a prince. But, if you can hold on to that lady, I'd be happy to escort Mrs. Pop. I can salsa, samba, and macarena."

"You got yourself a deal, Leo Leo Burrito," P. Pop said. "And next she says she wants to take acting lessons. Maybe get her own talk show."

"That sounds like great fun, P. Pop, but I don't know how much help I can be on that front. I don't know anyone on the talk show circuit." Leo pointed to Bounce Land and parked right in front. "Hey, can you get the kids outside for a birthday surprise?"

"Do you have the taxi? The Burrito Taxi?"

"I do, my man."

HONK!

"Did you hear that?" Leo asked. "That's me."

"I heard it. Hey kids! Want to see something cool?" There was a sound of yelling. "We are exiting the building now."

The line went dead for a second, then P. Pop came back on to the walkie. "Leo Burrito, get that lady off my Velcro wall."

"I'm on it," Leo said. To us he said, "You girls take care of ABJ, I'll bacon-up the kids."

We ran past the swarm of early-morning birthday party-goers on a vicious quest for bacon.

"I think I'm gonna have my birthday party in the morning before school," I said.

"I know. Right? And at a Bounce Land. I love this place."

"Or maybe the zoo."

"Or maybe an indoor water park."

Margot interrupted our rhythm, "These indoor bounce parks are like germ factories, people have been known to get mauled by tigers or lions at the zoo, and waterslides are a perfect way to get whiplash."

Payton said, "Well, you just sucked any potential for fun out of my birthday party."

We entered Bounce Land. While scanning the big warehouse I suggested, "Margot, maybe you can try not to look for the worst possible thing that can happen in a situation? We can help you."

"I like to point those things out to people who might not see them."

With the kids outside, the trampoline park was filled only with party music. Red plastic cups of orange juice covered the tables and countertops.

"That's considerate of you," I said to Margot. "But it kind of brings me down, sometimes."

"Really? Do you think that's why the kids at my school don't like me?"

"I'm sure the kids at your school like you," Payton said. "But it's possible that they don't want a black cloud over their head all the time."

There was a large bowl of fruit that looked untouched and a tray of small brown muffins.

"Let's start trying now," I said. "Think about rainbows."

Margot repeated, "Rainbows. Got it."

I broke off a piece of muffin and ate it. "These kids are lucky Leo bought burritos."

"Bad?" Payton asked.

"Bran. And it has raisins."

I asked, "What kind of a kid wants raisins at his birthday party?"

"Maybe the kind—"

A voice echoed off the warehouse walls. "Ah! Ha-ha!"

I knew that voice. It was ABJ. I looked across a lake of blue and black trampolines to see her one hundred percent inverted and stuck to a Velcro wall. Her blond hair was tangled and hung under her.

"That doesn't look good," Payton said. "Let's hurry."

28

"Hang on! We're coming, ABJ!" I called.

We bounced and bounced our way to her.

"Ah! Ha!" she called again.

Payton picked up Velcro-grabbing vests from a nearby hook. We put them on.

"Are you okay?" Payton asked ABJ.

"Okay? I'm great. Look at me!"

I had to laugh a little. "You aren't scared?"

"No way, José. You know I used to do my own stunts?"

"I didn't know that," I said.

"How did you get like that?" Margot asked.

"How else? I flipped!"

We looked at each other.

"One of you can go first," I said.

"That's okay," Margot said. "You can."

I put my hand behind my back. "One-two-three-shoot!"

Me: paper

Payton: scissors

Margot: a circle connecting her fingertips and thumb.

"What the heck is that?" I asked her.

"Lizard. You add a lizard when you play with three people." Margot explained, "Lizard beats scissors, and scissors cuts paper. So, Ginger, you lose."

"Did you just make that up?" I asked.

ABJ called down. "Everyone knows about lizard, Ginger!"

Maybe it was a West Coast thing. Anyway, I was going first.

"I've never done this before," I told Payton and Margot.

"How hard can it be?" Payton asked.

I backed up to a non-trampolined path, got a running start, then pounded both feet on a trampoline right under the Velcro wall. I made no attempt to flip. Really, I made no attempt at anything, and as a result—*SPLAT!*—arms out, legs out, face slap. I was splat, flat, face-first on the Velcro wall.

CLICK–swoop.

I asked Payton, "What are you doing?"

"QuickPik."

"Well, stop that."

"Sure thing."

My head was at ABJ's feet. My feet were at her head. She looked up at me; blood had rushed to her face. "Hi, there. Fun, isn't it?"

"It isn't going to be fun when Patel Poplawski calls the police," I said.

Payton reminded her, "You don't need another citation."

"And," I said, "they might be looking for us for impersonating a paranormal investigator."

Margot added, "And/or a British safety inspector."

"What?" ABJ asked. "What have you girls been doing?"

"Never mind," I said. "We've got to get you down."

"Or we could play on this wall," ABJ said.

"We have an important meeting with a bicycle cop, and we're going to be late," I said.

To Payton and Margot, she said, "Ginger is such a fuddy-duddy."

"I know. Right?"

"What?" I asked. "I am not!"

"Clearly, I'm the adventurous one," Payton said to me.

"We're exactly the same," I said. "We like the same clothes, like the same things, we both want to be doctors, and we know what the other will say. We're practically clones."

ABJ asked me, "You know she's black, right?"

"Okay. Besides that little detail, we're twins," I said. "Can we just get you down?"

"I thought about peeling myself loose," ABJ said. "But if I do, I'll fall on my head. And the doctor said that's not good for me."

"That's not recommended for anyone," Margot said. "Concussions are bad. They have long-term consequences on—"

"RAINBOWS!" Payton and I shouted at her.

"Rainbows?" ABJ asked.

"Right, rainbows." Then Margot suggested, "Maybe you can grab Ginger's feet and roll over onto your front. Then you can push off the Velcro."

"Good idea. And very rainbow-y," Payton said. Then she called to ABJ, "And we're right here."

ABJ took one of my ankles in each of her hands and rolled from her back to her front.

"That's good," Payton said. "Now, can you turn yourself around, so your feet are toward the floor, like Ginger?"

ABJ held my ankles with her hands and used her elbows

to push herself off the wall and reposition. She did this over and over until she and I made a perfect L. I was the up and down part, she was the sideways part.

"A few more times and your legs will practically be on the ground," Margot said. She repeated, "Rainbows," to herself.

ABJ was pulling on my legs with her weight. I could feel the Velcro on my belly between the wall and the vest coming loose.

"Hurry!" I said. "I can't hold on."

She pushed up with her elbows again, but this time she tugged at my feet a little too hard—

FFFFTTTT!!!!

My Velcro vest lost hold and we fell onto the trampoline below, missing Payton, but crushing Margot.

Oh no, I hope she didn't get a concussion.

"I'm okay," Margot groaned from underneath me. "Are you guys?"

ABJ swished her blond locks out of her face. "Great!"

There was the sound of applause. We looked up to see a party of eight-year-olds clapping for us.

P. Pop said, "And that concludes the entertainment portion of the party. The Velcro wall is now open!"

29

Leo delivered ABJ back to her house. Then, looking at his watch, he said, "We have forty-five minutes before we meet Mitch to check out that second *D*. And we have a bunch of burritos left."

"Where do you wanna park?" Payton asked.

"I have an idea that I think you two will like." Leo pulled over on the Sunset Strip in front of Crunch gym.

"Really?" I asked. "Are people going to eat bacon burritos after working out?"

"Once they smell these, they will," Payton said.

Margot added, "And these aren't just regular ordinary people."

We opened the trunk and the sweaty crowd exiting the

gym flocked to us. I realized right away what Leo meant about not "just regular ordinary people," when I recognized celebrity faces. Speaking of celebs, *hello, Emmit Hennessy*. He was the star of the last installment of the vampire trilogy.

"Good workout?" I asked him.

He grinned. "Super hot today." Then he winked at me!

I said, "Don't worry, your hypothalamus will regulate your temperature."

His smile faded, and he walked away. I was able to snap a pic of his back and—*swoop*—sent it to QuickPik.

Payton asked, "Seriously? *Hypothalamus*? Was that supposed to be cute?"

"Oh, just be quiet."

When Payton saw Jackson Holmes, who had just won an award, I think it was the Julio, for his part in *The Windblown Cornfield*, she said to him, "You might need two burritos."

"I do?" I asked.

"Yup. One for each of those guns."

Jackson smiled at the compliment and posed with the three of us for a selfie. *Swoop!* To QuickPik.

"Now, *that* was cute," Payton said to me after Jackson walked away.

"Sometimes when I get nervous, science comes out," I said.

Payton said, "We'll have to fix that before high school."

"Maybe you can think about rainbows too?" Margot suggested. "And that will relax you."

"Maybe," I said.

Even the ladies leaving Crunch gym took a burrito for the road. I recognized Tricia LaRock from *Shop Till You Drop Dead*. Payton and I weren't actually allowed to see that movie.

"Make sure you save two for Mitch," Leo said. "It was part of the deal."

Payton stashed six.

"We just need two," I said to her.

"I know, but watching all these people leaving the gym has built up my appetite. And I figured you guys would want one too."

"Good thinking," Margot said.

"I know. Right?"

Workers from a construction project across the street at The Laugh Factory spotted the Burrito Taxi, or smelled bacon, and cleaned us out.

"Perfect timing," Leo said. "Let's go find us a bicycle cop, a letter *D*, and a lost treasure."

30

"I cannot believe we saw Jackson Holmes," Payton said.

"He's even cuter in person," I said.

"It's been quite a morning," Leo said, careening the taxi up winding Mulholland Drive.

We found Mitch leaning against a shuttle bus, with his arms and legs crossed.

I popped out of the taxi first. I asked him, "You know what you look like you need?"

"A nap?"

"A burrito!"

"That's the next best thing to a nap," he said.

"This is better." Payton handed him two. "It's bacon!"

He bit into one and said, "You're right. It is better than

a nap." He pushed the rest of the burrito into his mouth. I think he said, "Let's go." Mitch continued talking through his food as he drove. Somehow Leo understood his muffled words. I think it was about the Wiener Mobile auction.

Ted swiped his passcard to open the razor-wire gate, and said to Payton and me, "I'm surprised you want to look here again."

"They realized there was another *D*," Margot said.

"In L-A-N-D," Payton said.

"Yeah. I should've thought of that."

As we got out of the shuttle, I asked, "Any chance you have a shovel or metal detector?"

"Nope," Mitch said. "But, don't forget, I have the power of the LAPD behind me. What else do you need?"

On the hike to the space where the last *D* in Hollywoodland had been, I explained what we were looking for to Mitch. "So, we need something to help us find and dig up a treasure chest."

Margot asked, "Could ABJ really dig a big hole and bring a treasure chest out here and bury it?"

"When you say it like that, it doesn't make sense," I said. "But this has to be the *D*. It totally makes sense with every part of the clue."

"Gimme just a second," Mitch said.

I took advantage of that second to take in the view from up here. I could see into the valley that was Hollywood, or maybe at one time, Hollywoodland. The hills were covered with green-brown trees ribboned with roads. Farther into the valley, the trees became more sparse, and the roads became straight, aligned into city blocks.

He mumbled as he tapped on his phone. "If I can get the GPS coordinates . . . got 'em. And I'll send them to my friend Sal from the NASA . . ."

"NASA? As in . . . NASA?" Payton asked. "You know someone there?"

"Sal and I were in the same LEGO League when we were kids. Out in Minnesota. We stay in touch on social media."

We made it to the spot. The ground was dry and hard. There was no way ABJ could dig a hole here. I walked around the area looking for a duffle bag of money. I didn't see one.

Margot put her hands on her hips. "Any word from NASA Sal from LEGO League?"

Mitch looked at his phone. "In fact there is." He held it out for us to see. "And it looks like good news."

"What are we looking at?" Leo asked.

"Thermal imaging from a satellite. Sal scanned the ground right where we are and guess what that is?" He pointed to a dark shape on the image on his phone.

"It's not a treasure chest," I said.

"Nope. It's a room." He walked a few steps using the phone to guide him. "It's right . . ." He took a few more steps then stopped. "Here." He started brushing leaves and dirt around with his feet until something appeared.

It was a handle. The metal color blended in with the colors of the earth.

Mitch kicked some more dirt away, and in just a minute I could make out the shape of a door. It was a door that I recognized—the same kind as the one in ABJ's kitchen closet.

"A fallout shelter," I said.

Mitch's radio made a *FFFFT!*

I tried to open the door the way I'd seen Leo do. It didn't budge.

Payton pointed to a twisting lock. "It has a combination."

Leo said, "We don't know what it is."

I felt a tingle in my brain. "I do," I said. "Four, thirty-six, ten."

Mitch asked, "How could you possibly know that?"

"It was on the clue." I took it out of my pocket. "See." I pointed to the hay bales of four short tick mark lines and one diagonal across.

"That's a way people count by fives," Payton explained. "ABJ did it when we inventoried her closet."

I spun the combination lock, and the door made a faint *pop* and a sigh.

Like ABJ's shelter, it was supplied with water, radios, blankets, canned food, flashlights, batteries, and there were piles of boxes. One small one in the middle of a stack was marked 1964–1966, the year missing from the boxes at ABJ's house.

Leo lifted the stuff on top of it and I slid it out.

I was covered with gooseflesh. It was cold in here, so maybe my hypothalamus needed a minute to regulate my body temperature, but I think it was the excitement.

"I can't stand it," Leo said. "The anticipation. The suspense. Open it up already!"

"Here we go," I said.

I remove the lid. There were stacks of hundred dollar bills tied together with paper marked $1,000.00, and then stacks of thousand dollar bills tied together with a marker that said $100,000.00. I added it together in my head. "More than one million dollars," I said.

"Exactly one million and twenty thousand," Payton corrected me.

"And—" Margot reached down to a Christmas gift bag on the floor.

"Is it eight and a half pounds?" I asked.

Payton held it. "Eeeeexactly." She pulled out the statue. "One Oscar."

"Priceless," Leo said.

"I know. Right?" I exclaimed.

31

ABJ recognized the box immediately when we brought everything in. "You found it!"

"What?" Dad asked.

"ABJ's money," I said.

"And an Oscar." Payton handed it to her.

"Where was it?" Mom asked.

"Temporarily misplaced," I said.

"Banking error," Payton said.

"Purely an accident," Margot said.

"Happens all the time," Mitch said.

Mom asked Mitch, "Who are you?"

"Mitch LaBleu." He pointed to his badge with one hand

and extended the other one for handshakes. "Bicycle cop. B-Nineteen."

"And—" Leo encouraged Mitch to say more.

"And the proud owner of a Wiener Mobile."

"You're kidding?" Dad asked.

"Nope. I just picked it up," Mitch added.

"Can I see it?" Grant, who wore his familiar football helmet with tin foil balls, asked.

"Sure," Mitch said. "But what's with all this?" He referred to the helmet.

"I'm expecting a call," Grant said. "Can't wait to tell them all about the Wiener Mobile. Can I go for a ride?"

"Sure can."

Then to ABJ, Mitch said, "By the way, it's a pleasure to meet you. I'm a huge fan."

"Aren't you sweet."

Dad, Grant, and Mitch went to the street to see the Wiener Mobile.

"I have to see this," Mom said. "I'll call the bank later to get this sorted out."

"I took care of that, Mom," I said.

"You did?"

"Yep," I said. "I told them we can't use them anymore."

"She was quite polite about it," Margot said.

"I said that we were going to bank somewhere else."

Payton clarified, "*Elsewhere* was the word she used."

"Well, good job. You girls are getting very mature," Mom said. "I'm going to check out the wiener."

When it was just me, Payton, and Margot, I said to ABJ, "It was at the *D* in Hollywoodland."

"In a bomb shelter up there," Payton said.

"Hollywoodland, of course. That's the bomb shelter that Howard Hughes built. It was a big secret. Only a few select people in the inside circle of Hollywood fame knew about it. You know, in case we needed a place to go." She sighed. "I was in the inside circle back then. And that is a special place to me. I went there with Clint Eastwood."

"To kiss?" I asked.

"Usually to run lines in private. But, yeah," she said. "We kissed once too."

"That area is totally restricted now. How did you get there?"

"I get fan mail. And sometimes I write back. One guy who wrote to me works at the radio tower and offered to bring me there to reminisce," she explained. "I brought a shoebox and my Oscar. When my pen pal gave me a minute to be alone, I went in—I remembered the combination, can you believe it, after all these years? And I hid my stuff among the other boxes."

"And you wrote yourself a note," I said.

"Good thing that you did," Margot said.

"Good thing you girls came out here to help me. Now I can stay in my house. How can I thank you?"

"I have a few ideas," I said.

"It's for the Science Olympics," Payton added.

"Anything to get those DeMarcos," ABJ said.

32

There were just twenty-four hours left in Hollywood, and Payton, Margot, and I had a lot of ground to cover to get my grand plan in motion.

First we went to the Hollywood Chamber of Commerce, where we filled out an application for a very special surprise for ABJ.

Next we met with ABJ's doctor to talk about Alzheimer's disease over a snack. Turned out that he loved burritos.

Then we dared to return to the Dolby Theatre.

"You!" Harry said when he saw us. "You aren't allowed in here. Do you know how much trouble I got in for canceling that tour? I got a demotion!"

"Just hear us out," I said.

We apologized to Harry and presented him with an amazing opportunity.

Last we went to see Patel Poplawski at Bounce Land. We only went there to talk, but ended up bouncing and jumping onto a Velcro wall for two hours.

Who says I'm a fuddy-duddy?

When we returned to ABJ's house late that afternoon, Mom asked, "Where have you been?"

"Everywhere," Margot said.

"You know, a lot to do with the Olympics," I said.

"And another little project we're working on," Payton added.

"Hey, Dad, I need to talk to you about an idea. An invention. I really think this could be TBO."

33

"Bacon burritos!" Margot called as she walked in the front door.

"Get 'em while they're hot!" Leo said.

"We're out here," ABJ called from the patio where she sat with Payton and me.

We'd had a chance to fill her in on everything, and she loved the plans.

Once the bacon smell infiltrated the house, we were joined by Grant, Mom, and Dad.

Dad opened a foil wrapper. "Perfect for our last morning."

"I'm gonna miss this when we get back to Delaware," Mom said.

Grant pulled out a ziplock bag filled with small leftover bites of a week's worth of burritos. "I saved these. To send to my people."

"Gross," I said.

"Eeew," Payton said.

"How are you going to get it to them?" Leo asked.

"I'm gonna flush it down the airplane toilet and when it shoots out the back of the plane, there won't be a gravitational pull and it will float in space until discovered."

I didn't want to tell him that planes didn't let poop fly into space, because other than that, it was a clever idea. Weird, but clever.

"Rainbows. Rainbows. Rain—I can't rainbow this one, sorry." Margot explained to Grant, "Exposing alien life to Earthly bacteria will make them very sick, which will make them very mad. When they feel better they'll probably attack and annihilate our whole planet."

"That's a great point." Grant threw the leftover food away.

"I guess everything can't be rainbows all the time," I said to Margot.

Payton said, "I'm so glad I met you, or I never would have known there were so many possible natural disasters in the world."

"I know I'll do anything in my power never to get a splinter," I agreed. "So, thanks for that."

"You're welcome," Margot said. "This was the best spring break I've ever had."

We high-butted.

Then I hugged ABJ. "This was a great visit. Thanks for the adventure."

"No. Thank you for you-know-what."

"What?" Mom asked.

"If I wanted you to know, I wouldn't have said you-know-what," ABJ said. Then to Payton she said, "I hope you'll come again."

"I know. Right? Me too."

Grant said to ABJ, "You're okay for an Earthling."

ABJ said, "And you're okay for an alien."

"Gee, thanks. No one's ever said that to me before." Grant glowed with delight.

Later in the day, Leo loaded the Science Olympics project and luggage into ABJ's Caddy.

He honked and we waved the whole way as we drove down her street.

34

⚘

One Week Later
Delaware Middle School Science Olympics

Mrs. Walsh strolled around the school gymnasium and scribbled notes on her clipboard. Finally, she came to our display: HEALTHY BRAIN AFFECTED BY ALZHEIMER'S DISEASE.

I started our presentation, "Welcome to our exhibit. On this table you will see a model of a healthy brain. It weighs about three pounds. Specific regions of the cortex interpret sensations, solve problems, generate thoughts, store memories, and control involuntary movements."

Payton said, "You will see that those regions are labeled."

"The brain has more than one hundred billion neurons. Signals traveling through the neurons control thoughts, feelings, and memories."

Payton pointed. "You will see here that the neurons are represented by these white Christmas lights."

I led us into the *ooh la la* portion of the presentation, "Alzheimer's disease destroys these neurons."

Payton pushed the button and half of the Christmas lights went out.

We paused.

I noticed Mrs. Walsh write something down.

I said, "This affects all of the brain's functions."

Payton said, "People afflicted with Alzheimer's disease will suffer nerve cell death and tissue loss, causing the organ to shrink dramatically."

And now, for the *kapow*.

Payton lifted a veil that covered the second brain of our project. It looked very different from the first one.

I said, "This is what a brain affected by Alzheimer's disease looks like."

There were oohs and aahs. *Hello, kapow.*

Payton said, "You will see the cortex has shriveled up, and the hippocampus has shrunk."

I used a laser pointer to direct the audience's eyes to our final poster. "You will see here in pictures from a doctor in California, various images of the brain in varying states of decomposition."

Payton said, "The speed of progression of Alzheimer's disease varies greatly. In addition to medications, individuals can help slow the development of the disease by doing these four things: maintaining physical activity; eating healthy; continually having mental challenges; and frequently socializing with other people."

"Alzheimer's disease has a devastating effect on individuals and families," I said. "As the disease gets worse, people may not recognize loved ones, or be able to take care of themselves."

Together Payton and I both said, "Thank you for looking at our presentation of how Alzheimer's disease affects a healthy brain and what people can do to slow the progression."

Our friends, teachers, family, and competitors clapped and we bowed.

Mrs. Walsh didn't say anything. She simply nodded, wrote on her clipboard, and progressed to the next project.

Payton whispered to me, "Two words: *kapow.*"

Finally Mrs. Walsh reached the DeMarcos.

Victor DeMarco explained how they'd made a robot out of parts from a Roomba vacuum cleaner, a blender, and an old record player.

His twin, Wyatt DeMarco, pushed a button to show how their robot could dance. A figure made out of Play-Doh, dressed in a tuxedo, bow tie, and top hat, spun around on the record player's turntable. Then it rode around on the Roomba, which Wyatt controlled with a remote.

"And now for the big finale," Victor said. He tossed a tomato, an onion, and a clove of garlic into the robot's top hat, where they were blended up.

Wyatt returned the robot to its starting place, opened a bag of tortilla chips, and dipped one into the top hat. "Salsa," he said.

The kids clapped and cheered and helped themselves to chips and dip.

"Appetizers?!" I asked Payton as we waited for the winner to be announced.

"Seriously?" Payton asked. "How can we compete with *appetizers?*"

"You know what we should have given away?" I asked.

"Kittens!" we both said.

Mrs. Walsh stood at the microphone at the front of the gymnasium. "Clearly science can be fun; and I encourage fun."

Mrs. Walsh was about the most un-fun teacher at our school, but whatever.

"But I applaud the team that took this Science Olympics to a seriously personal level and educated us all on the devastating effects of an all-too-common illness," she said as she rested her clipboard on her thighs. "I have no doubt that this year's first place winners are Payton Paterson and Ginger Carlson. Great job, girls."

We won!

We bumped our hips together.

"Get to it, twins," Payton said.

"A bet's a bet," I added.

We followed the DeMarcos to the front of the school, where they tossed their jeans and oxfords into a pile and ran around the football field in their boxer shorts.

I took a picture of the pile of clothes and—*swoop*—posted it on QuickPik, because if it wasn't on QuickPik, it was like it never really happened.

35

"We won," I told ABJ over the phone. I filled her in on all the details. "Are you ready for the big ceremony?"

She said, "I don't know if I can do it."

"What? Why? You've waited forever for this."

"I know. But I am so nervous. I haven't done a big event in such a long time. Maybe it would be different if you were here."

On the way to the luggage carousel at LAX, I passed a TV in the airport. The commercial caught my eye. "Payt, check it out."

It was a commercial for my dad's latest gadget. The official spokesperson was Harry, from the Dolby. Once he and

Dad started working on the prototype, he resigned and now he works full-time for Dad.

Harry on the TV was saying, "If you're anything like me, you like to wear your pants up high." Harry hiked up his pants and secured them there by tightening his belt. "But this can cause discomfort." He turned to show the audience his wedgie.

Then Patel Poplawski from Bounce Land walked into the commercial and said, "You know what you need, my main man? The Anti-Wedgie Pad." P. Pop held up Dad's invention. It was a soft plastic mold in the shape of a butt. He said, "I'm wearing one right now, which is why I don't have a wedgie." P. Pop turned around and showed the viewers the seat of his pants: no wedgie.

The next frame of the commercial showed Harry's smooth butt. "I love the Anti-Wedgie Pad."

Leo and Mitch loaded our luggage into their cars. They'd brought the Wiener Mobile, which had been redesigned to look just like the Burrito Taxi, and the Caddy. Dad, Mom, and Grant drove in the Caddy with Mitch, whose police bicycle hung off a rack attached to the trunk. Payton and me went with Leo and Margot.

"You wanna?" Margot indicated the Wiener Mobile's plexiglass sidecar.

I asked, "Really?"

She nodded.

I climbed in. As she was sliding the door shut, she said, "If you feel like you are going to suffocate, just think about rainbows."

"Good advice." I smiled at the sight of palm trees, Sunset Boulevard, and Sunset Tower.

"ABJ should be home about the same time as us."

I heard Leo through the headphones. "Where is she?" I asked into the little wire microphone that I had bent in front of my mouth.

"Getting her hair done with Mrs. Poplawski for the big event. Since you suggested that they go dancing together, they've become best friends. Now ABJ is giving her acting lessons."

"That's great," I said. "I'm so glad that she's socializing with friends."

"And exercising," Payton said.

"Oh, she loves it," Leo said. "She's also been helping me with my new healthy menu and with advertising." He pointed out the front window at a billboard. It was a picture of the burrito fleet: the original Burrito Taxi, the Wiener Mobile, and the Caddy. The Caddy wasn't dressed up like a burrito, but it was covered with magnetic advertisements on every side. ABJ was the customer on the billboard. She looked just like Marilyn Monroe would have if she were thirty years older and biting into a vegetarian, whole-wheat burrito.

"I love it," I said.

"I know. Right?" Payton said.

Margot said, "The new line of healthy burritos has really taken off."

"Awesome," I said about the increased burrito business, and also about my first glimpse of the Hollywood sign. "How has ABJ been feeling?" I asked Leo.

"She takes her medicine and follows the routine that you worked out with her doctor. Harry installed an alarm, and now he's renting a room upstairs. We got him a walkie too, so she has a whole network of people available to her at the push of a button."

"Great news," Payton said.

"That's right. All rainbows in Hollywood," Margot said. "With just a touch of smog, not enough to cause a cough or wheeze. You hardly notice it because it's really all about the rainbows."

Margot had made a lot of progress, and I was proud of her.

Leo asked, "Do you girls want to pick up ABJ's dress?"

Payton said, "You know it."

Leo drove past the Beverly Wilshire Hotel, down Rodeo Drive to Dior. Thanks to Grace Taggart, the mannequins in the windows were modeling the Anti-Wedgie Pad.

Grace had ABJ's dress waiting for us at the counter.

"Cheer-io," she said to us.

"Cheerios to you," I said. "How've you been?"

"All your precautions in order?" Margot asked with a laugh.

"Wait. Your accents! You're *not* British!" Grace said. "I didn't think so."

"Nope," I said.

"And I figured you made up the whole SIREN thing too."

"And you still let us snoop around?"

"Sure," she said. "I thought it was all pretty funny."

"You're a good sport," I said. "Well, do you have it?"

"Ta-da!" Grace held up the dress she had designed especially for Betty-Jean Bergan.

"She'll love it!" Payton said.

"It's perfect," Margot added.

Grace handed us the dress. "See you tonight."

36

‿‿‿

Paparazzi snapped our pictures as white-gloved concierges helped us out of our fleet of vehicles. ABJ was the last to get out. She looked amazing in a long black silk dress and matching boa. She, Payton, Margot, and I all wore the same shoes: pink sneakers!

We followed her down Hollywood Boulevard to an area blocked off with red velvet rope. ABJ paused and smiled for the cameras like the pro that she was.

"Do you have anything you'd like to say?" a French reporter named Murielle DuPluie called to her.

"I would," she said. "I now consider myself part of Hollywood history. I want to thank the selection committee for choosing me. It is an honor to have my own star on the Walk of Fame."

After the ceremony we went to Millions of Milkshakes, where I stole a private minute with ABJ. "You look really happy."

"I am, Ginger."

"There's something I wanted you to know. We have a great bedroom in Delaware just waiting for you, whenever you want it."

She hugged me.

"Oh, I want one too," Payton said, rushing over.

"Me too!" Margot said.

ABJ hugged us all.

P. Pop delivered shakes to all of my weird friends and family: my brother in an aluminum foil helmet, two burrito-taxi drivers, an Anti-Wedgie Pad inventor and its official model/spokesperson, a classic movie nut, a Bounce Land manager, and his salsa-dancing mother.

I had a thought. *Am I weird too?*

Are Payton and I science-y, pink sneaker-y, and maybe paranormal investigator-y impersonating weirdos?

My brain tingled and I smiled at the answer, then I held up my shake. "To ABJ!" I cried, and everyone repeated after me.

Then we all sipped our shakes through Millions of Milkshakes' new signature straw—a Twizzler!

Turn the page for a sneak peek
at Cindy's next book:
Sydney Mackenzie Knocks 'Em Dead

Even though I hated vampires and just about anything scary, I'd seen *Fangs for You* five times.

"I loved it more than last week," my best friend, Leigh, said.

"Me too," I agreed. "Emiline was amazing. Totally amazing!" I dreamed of being exactly like fifteen-year-old Hollywood sweetheart Emiline Hunt some day. Some day soon. I could see it now: I walk down the red carpet, blinded by camera flashes. My name is in big, bright lights—FANGS FOR ME: STARRING SYDNEY MACKENZIE.

Back in the real world, Leigh and I pushed open the tinted-glass door of the Regal Cinema LA.

"So, what now?" Leigh asked.

"You know what would make this day even more perfect? If we went for some frozi yogi!"

"Yes!" Leigh said. "*That* is a fab idea. Let's do it. As in, right now."

So we walked to Martucci's, our favorite place for fab frozi yogi. They always had *the* best flavors. Today it was California Colada, Leigh's fave, and Satiny Red Velvet Cake, my ultimate. As we walked I checked my phone for messages.

That is when the unthinkable happened. A kid on a skateboard bumped into me and knocked my phone out of my hand. It crashed to the ground and broke in three pieces.

[Pause for dramatic effect.]

"Sorry," he called as he boarded away. But sorry wasn't going to help. I'd spent a month secretly cat-sitting to earn enough money for that phone!

"No biggie," Leigh said. Of course it wasn't a biggie to Leigh. She had her dad's gold Amex for "emergencies." I carried around my mom's expired card. "We'll go to the Apple store after this and get you a new one."

"That's okay, I want the new iPhone that isn't out yet," I lied. "I have to have it."

"Oh yeah. Me too," she said. "But what will you use until then?"

I held the three pieces. "This doesn't look bad. Jim can probably fix it." Jim is my dad and he is the most un-handy person in the world.

"If he can't, I think I have my old one in a drawer some-where. You can totally have it." Leigh was always sharing her stuff with me.

Leigh forgot about my phone, but I continued to worry that I'd be a social outcast, which was something I couldn't afford.

We got our yogurt and ate at an outside table and pored over the latest issue of *Teen Dream* magazine, the one with Emiline Hunt on the cover.

Leigh pointed to a dress. "Your strappy Guess sandals would look good with that."

"Totally." The sandals weren't actually Guess. Leigh had assumed they were and I didn't correct her. They *looked* like Guess.

I glanced at my watch. (Actually it was my mom's.) "I have to get home. Our yoga instructor is coming to the house at five." It was really Roz's (aka my mom's) yoga instructor.

I managed to untangle myself from my web of lies to grab a bus home after another day in my sunny, silver-screeny, thrilling, frozi yogi, medium-popular world in Southern California.

I'm not one to exaggerate, but my parents tried to ruin my life. It started after the yogurt.

I ran into the cream-colored stucco house. "Roz! I'm home and I have a serious problem."

What if someone is trying to text me right now? I don't know who, but someone might be.

I did a double-take when I saw Roz and Jim Mackenzie hanging out in the living room. Roz sat on the light tan leather couch, her hands in tight fists in her lap. Jim paced across the Oriental rug, back and forth in front of the piano that no one played.

Am I in trouble for something?

I recalled the recent torture I'd inflicted on my twin

six-year-old brothers. But I didn't think it was bad enough to result in a lecture from both Roz *and* Jim.

"We have to talk to you about something," Roz said. "Sit down."

Jim's forehead wrinkled. "We've sold the sporting goods stores."

"Okay. Why? Where are you gonna work?"

"We were losing money. In fact, we lost a lot of money." Based on the fact that I had to cat-sit for a month to make enough money for a cell phone, I figured we couldn't afford to lose a lot of money.

Roz said, "We're going to make some changes."

"Like what?" *Am I going to be phone-less or homeless?*

"Some very difficult, very big changes." Her tone told me we were heading toward homeless.

"We're thinking about this family's future," Jim continued. "We need to make more money, and spend less—a lot less."

Roz made an effort to mutter, "And *save* more." Like me, Roz preferred spending to saving.

Jim's expression lightened and he began to look more like the glass-is-half-full kinda guy I knew. "So we're starting a new business! One that booms regardless of the economy."

"A yogurt boutique?"

They shook their heads.

"People aren't always going to buy expensive clothes or go out to eat," Jim explained. "We want a business that's 'recession proof.'" He made air quotes with his fingers.

"What's 'recession proof'?" I copied his quotes.

"You see, Sydney," Roz began. "As sad as it is, people are always going to die. And they need a place . . . er . . . what I mean is, they need to go to a . . ."

Jim jumped in, "What your mother is trying to say is that we've inherited a cemetery. That's going to be our new family business."

Did you LOVE reading this book?

Visit the Whyville...

Where you can:

◯ Discover great books!

◯ Meet new friends!

◯ Read exclusive sneak peeks and more!

Log on to visit now!
bookhive.whyville.net

IF YOU ♥ THIS BOOK,
you'll love all the rest from

YOUR HOME AWAY FROM HOME:

AladdinMix.com

HERE YOU'LL GET:

- ♥ The first look at new releases
- ♥ Chapter excerpts from all the Aladdin M!X books
- ♥ Videos of your fave authors being interviewed

Aladdin ♥ Simon & Schuster Children's Publishing

Check out these great titles from Aladdin M!X:

ALADDINMIX.COM